FOUR
CORE
FICTION

FOUR CORE FICTION

A STORY GRID EDITION
SHORT STORY ANTHOLOGY

STORY GRID

A STORY GRID EDITION: 0002
STORY GRID PUBLISHING LLC

STORY GRID

Story Grid Publishing, LLC
223 Egremont Plain Road
PMB 191
Egremont, MA 01230

Goliath Approaches by Leslie Watts, edited by Rachelle Ramirez

The Confession by Tim Grahl, edited by Valerie Francis

Outpost 5 by J. Thorn, edited by Ira Heinichen

Let Justice Prevail by Mark McGinn, edited by Leslie Watts

X Pass by Rebekah Olson, edited by Randall Surles

High Plains Migration by Shelley Sperry, edited by Larry Pass

I Brush My Teeth Left-Handed and Other Reasons You Should Date Me by Rebecca Monterusso,
Edited by Danielle Kiowski

Jaws by Courtney Harrell, edited by Melanie Naumann

Above All Else by Shawn Coyne, edited by Tim Grahl

The Good Daughter by Rachelle Ramirez, edited by Anne Hawley

An Artist's Test by Kimberly Kessler, edited by Abigail K. Perry

Elixir by Julia Blair, edited by Catherine Lunardon

Cover Design by Magnus Rex
Produced and Globally Edited by
Kimberly Kessler and Rebecca Monterusso

First Story Grid Publishing Paperback Edition
May 2020

For Information about Special Discounts for Bulk Purchases,
Please Visit www.storygridpublishing.com

ISBN: 978-1-64501-019-7
eBook: 978-1-64501-020-3

For All Past, Present, and Future Story Nerds

ABOUT THIS ANTHOLOGY

Four Core Fiction is a set of short stories, one per global content genre, written by Story Grid Certified Editors and based on the Story Grid micro-skill-focused "Ground Your Craft" course from Summer School 2019.

The goal of that course (and this subsequent anthology) is to teach writers how to craft the all-important Core Event scene using masterworks as a guide.

In GYC, Shawn Coyne, the founder of Story Grid methodology, analyzes a short story/chapter that represents the Core Event scene for each of the twelve content genres. For each masterwork story/scene, he shows the underlying structure by delineating the beat-by-beat progression. The micro value shifts happening within each beat produce the scene's overall structure and the global change of the scene.

He then extrapolates an abstract framework from the beats that can be used to create a wholly new story. It's similar to the process by which Joseph Campbell sussed out the Hero's Journey archetypal structure but on a micro-level. Using these abstract frameworks, each of the Story Grid Certified Editor contributors created an original story using complementary beats and narrative devices as their inspiring masterwork scenes.

We've discovered that this process not only teaches writers the mindset of other successful storytellers, but it enables them to complete the blue-collar work necessary to create a Core Event scene that works.

Writing a story is an act of vulnerability, and if you're genuinely trying to grow your craft, it's never not scary. But one of the greatest gifts of GYC, and learning to study and apply masterworks in this way, is the value of constraints.

Writer's block (aka Resistance) happens when we don't know what to do next. But when we embrace constraints—in this case, specifically a beat-by-beat progression taken from a masterwork— we have a guide to follow. From there, we have the freedom to create and even innovate original pieces of literary art.

In the Story Grid Universe, we wholeheartedly embrace blue-collar work. We hope that by reading these stories and perhaps the companion guide that details the process by which we wrote them, you will get a clearer understanding of what comes from doing that work yourself.

TABLE OF CONTENTS

FOUR CORE FICTION

ACTION

GOLIATH APPROACHES

Written by Leslie Watts
Edited by Rachelle Ramirez

Captain Lawford first sensed *Goliath's* approach while sitting at the compact desk in her cabin where she reviewed the daily dispatch of engagements and sightings. Lawford felt as if she were falling, though no movement of the ship, and she knew something was not right.

Her ship was one of six to leave Firion the morning before— five decoys, each flying the queen's standard, and her own HMS *Convert*, which bore no standard but carried Tulland's new queen. The Admiralty's aim had been to confuse their enemies while transporting Queen Lenore to the capital for coronation after her mother's death. Lawford read with particular interest the portion of the dispatch that described a pattern of events along and near the northerly sea lanes between Port Firion and Tulland.

Grabbing her glass, she scanned the horizon through her cabin window. A red flash sprouted in the distance and raced toward her. The pirate ship *Goliath* had found them.

The lookout cried, "Red sails, ho!"

Lieutenant Parker, HMS *Convert*'s XO, called from the quarterdeck, "Beat to quarters! Beat to quarters!" The ship's inhabitants sprang to life.

The red sails of the Rafolk were always cause for alarm, and Lawford knew the ship hunting them was the worst of its kind. To the familiar rhythm of the drum, she made her way to the quarterdeck.

Lawford inspected the red ship as it flew across the water toward them. Illegible black writing on the sails would, on closer inspection, proclaim Edward Lough's motto, "Woe to the vanquished." Lough, *Goliath*'s captain and the bloodthirsty leader of Rafolk would be on them in an hour's time. Lawford could just make out Lough's form on his own quarterdeck, towering over the queen's uncle, Denholm, who had joined the Rafolk in an attempt to seize power during the transition.

"It's *Goliath*, Captain," Parker said.

"Yes, Lieutenant," the captain replied. "Let's clear the deck for action."

Parker turned, shouting orders and doing all that could and should be done, from stowing boats to putting out lanterns. Lawford observed these preparations while considering which course to take.

It was said that Lough could bend the ocean currents and winds to his will. He had seized or sunk hundreds of ships throughout the common sea lanes. The pirate was clever, but his gift was that of shipscraft, not seacraft, and the legend of Lough was down to his ship.

Goliath was formidable with 124 guns and crews that could fire salvos in under two minutes. But even this wasn't that remarkable. Plenty of ships carried as many powerful guns and well-trained crews. Despite its uniform red appearance, the ship consisted of a collection of salvaged boards from veteran ships Lough had defeated or otherwise obtained, a practice that integrated the collective knowledge and experience of each vessel. As a result, *Goliath*'s captain and crew didn't need to be particularly skilled in seacraft, and they needed only a few hands to navigate and fire. The ship made up for most deficits, so long as the pirates stayed out of the way. Having read the accounts of the pirate ship's exploits, Lawford had no reason to doubt this.

HMS *Convert* would lose a cannon fight. The battle might last all of fifteen minutes, maybe fewer, once they were in range and fully engaged. Lawford's best chance, she knew, was to neutralize *Goliath*'s advantage. Lawford could see no way to lure him near enough to board without being sunk first. Her Tulland marines and crew could overcome the undisciplined pirates in hand-to-hand fighting, if only she could get them aboard. But Lough's ship had never been boarded, and the pirate knew better than to let HMS *Convert* get close. He could sink her from a safe distance and pick off the survivors, ensuring the queen never reached the capital.

And though lighter and more agile, HMS *Convert* couldn't out-run *Goliath*, not at the rate the red ship was gaining. Lawford eyed the sun's position. It was early evening, but darkness would not fall in time for them to slip into the dark, and there was no fog. Favorable winds wouldn't benefit either ship in a chase, and under the circumstances, flight would buy her minutes but nothing more.

Given time, she knew she could access a viable alternative, but HMS *Convert* would be within the range of *Goliath*'s guns soon. The five o'clock bell sounded, and the watch called out the ship's position. Lawford thought of the dispatches she'd read and heaved a worried sigh. Well, this would have to do, and it just might.

Just then, she spotted Queen Lenore on the stern deck. Lawford strode to where the queen stood with her guards. "Your Majesty, we need to get you below."

"Lough and Denholm will already have spotted me. It won't make a difference now. What is your plan?"

"I'm sure you're right, but we can't risk a lucky shot by a musket-wielding pirate." Lawford indicated the ladder to guide the queen below.

The queen didn't move. "You do have a plan, Captain?"

"The beginnings of one, yes."

"Will you tell me?"

Lawford considered and then said, "It's a bit premature, but I'll let you know as soon as I can. Your Majesty, your cooperation is most appreciated." Lawford gestured toward the ladder again.

The queen sighed and descended the ladder, followed by her guards. With the queen tucked away below, Lawford prepared to leverage every possible advantage for their inevitable collision with *Goliath*.

"Ms. Cochrane, new heading, turn us south."

"South?" the helmswoman questioned and then caught herself. "Aye, Captain." She turned the wheel and then held it steady. Cochrane called out the new course once attained.

Lieutenant Parker approached Lawford and spoke quietly. "Forgive my presumption, Captain. We can't outrun *Goliath*, and in this direction, we'll hit the south winds soon and drift on the Adamantine current. Won't that play into Lough's hand? Perhaps we'd have a better chance if we turn and fight now. It's not what he would expect."

Lawford nodded. "I'm aware of our proximity to the Adamantine Reef and the risk of drift. Despite the difficulties presented, I trust that the officers, marines, and crew will do their duty."

"Yes, Captain." The lieutenant was not fully satisfied but, under the circumstances, would not press her objection further.

As Parker predicted, within forty-five minutes, HMS *Convert* lost speed in the weak southerly winds and drifted, allowing *Goliath* to close the distance between the ships. Cannon fire erupted from *Goliath*. Following the first shot, the pirates fired regularly, though HMS *Convert* was still out of range. The pirates would have plenty of ammunition and wouldn't mind spending it to taunt and wear down Lawford's crew. It wouldn't have the desired effect. Not yet.

Lawford turned her glass toward *Goliath* again. Lough and Denholm shared matching grins. No doubt the inadequate flight of HMS *Convert* amused them. Lawford needed to stay the course and hold her nerve.

Minutes later, HMS *Convert* rocked with the impact of the first direct hits. Cannon shot bounced along the deck as the starboard rail shattered and splinters flew, one of which struck the captain's face. Bits of the ship rained down on Lawford, but she wiped the sweat from her face and regained her footing. As the debris settled, the officers around her assumed their former positions.

Lawford yelled to the quartermaster, who was inspecting the stern deck, "Damage report, Ms. Maitland?"

"No dead, Captain, though several are injured," Maitland said. "A few substantial hits. Two guns were knocked off their carriages. The carpenters are seeing to the repairs now."

"Thank you, Ms. Maitland." They'd been lucky not to lose any crew members, but how long would that state hold?

Cannon fire continued with more direct hits to the rigging and superstructure. The rank smell of cannon smoke tainted the air. The officers grew restless, shifting their weight from side to side and gazing about the deck. Lawford caught the XO's eye and exaggerated the action of straightening her back. Mentioning the need to maintain their demeanor would only embarrass the officers in front of the crew and undermine their focus.

Parker stepped slowly with her hands behind her back to Lawford's side. "Captain, we continue to drift. Do you have additional orders for us?"

Lawford opened her mouth to respond but spotted a runner coming full speed toward them.

"Captain," the boy said out of breath, "an Auvergnat ship has been spotted dead ahead. We were all focused on *Goliath*..."

"Never mind that now. Thank you. Back to your post."

Lawford turned to see an Auvergnat war ship making straight for them just as the ship fired a warning toward HMS *Convert*.

Inconstante, it had to be.

Yesterday's dispatch reported she'd been patrolling the edge of their territory. Though they were at war with the Auvergnat, Lawford assumed the presence of their mutual enemy might afford an impromptu joint venture. Parker and the other officers were visibly deflated. A second enemy ship would finish them all the faster.

"Hard to starboard, Ms. Cochrane!" Captain Lawford yelled. Cochrane confirmed the order and spun the great wheel to turn the ship. "Take heart, Lieutenant Parker. Let's signal *Inconstante*."

Parker ran off to see it done while Lawford watched the Auvergnat ship's captain through her glass. Within moments of HMS *Convert's* turn, Captain de Naumann had clearly spotted the signal and the larger threat. She nodded, Lawford assumed not for her benefit, but in acknowledgment of the situation. De Naumann yelled orders to her officers and crew. *Inconstante* adjusted course to attack *Goliath*.

On return, Parker said, "Well, I'll be damned."

"Perhaps not today, Lieutenant." The captain smiled briefly. "Get us out of range of *Goliath's* guns, Ms. Cochrane."

"Aye, Captain." The helmswoman continued turning the ship to the north.

Lawford studied the receding conflict. Soon, *Inconstante's* starboard broadside faced *Goliath*. Lawford admired the skill and speed with which Captain de Naumann maneuvered the great ship and the way her crew responded to her. They acted as one body, rather than hundreds of individuals.

Of all the captains of the Auvergnat fleet to appear, Lawford couldn't have wished for a better one. She had seen de Naumann as commander of a smaller ship, the *Dauphine*. It was a different time, when the two nations fought together against the pirates that endangered the common sea lanes before differences led to hostilities between the former allies. Now, at the helm of *Inconstante* with its 120 guns and disciplined crew, she might carry the day against *Goliath*.

The pirate crew, though clearly surprised at first, was undaunted by the Auvergnat ship. Lough swaggered across the deck, still grinning. Perhaps he counted on disabling and seizing the remains of *Inconstante* to repair any damage the Auvergnat ship might inflict. Then he would chase and sink HMS *Convert*. In his mind, conquest would be delayed, not denied.

Lough grabbed the wheel from his helmsman and shouted orders to the crew. He relied on his ship to find the ideal approach, and *Goliath* adjusted position to swing the port broadside to face *Inconstante*. *Goliath* fired first, and the Auvergnat ship responded with her own broadside. But *Goliath* fired another full salvo. Lough knew how to leverage his assets. His men could fling hot iron quickly and repeatedly.

Inconstante fired half salvos with time between to line up further shots and make the most of every gun. De Naumann aimed for precision and accuracy, rather than blunt force. She fired less often, but her shots hit home. Even so, the pirate ship lost no speed or maneuverability. The hull seemed impervious to cannon fire.

The battle continued in this way until smoke, combined with weak winds and dusk, clouded Lawford's view. *Inconstante* must have sustained significant damage because the pirate guns never seemed to stop. The last action she saw was a nasty shot below *Inconstante*'s water line. Alone, it was not enough to sink her, but crewmembers would have to pump water for the duration of the battle, drawing them away from the guns. Blunt force would win out over precision, and the pirates would sink the Auvergnat ship soon.

Lawford could slip away.

Though she had brought the pirate to de Naumann's front door, and honor dictated that she provide assistance, her primary duty was clear. Queen Lenore needed to arrive safely in the capital. It would be dark by the time the battle was over, but their destination and route were no longer secret. It might be close, but in all likelihood, *Goliath* would be on them again before they could reach home.

"Cochrane, turn us about and back into the fight. Lieutenant Parker, get the sharpshooters into the rigging. Have the gun crews load the carronades with grapeshot. Form up the rest of the marines along the rail and prepare all nonessential officers and crew to board. Distribute pikes, cutlasses, bayonets, and knives from the mess if you need to. All hands not otherwise engaged should have a weapon and line up behind the marines."

Parker nodded at something over Lawford's shoulder.

"Does that include me?"

Lawford turned to find the queen dressed in a borrowed officer uniform with a regulation sword hanging from her belt. Her guards, similarly disguised and armed, flanked the monarch.

"Your Majesty, the Auvergnat ship, *Inconstante*, has engaged *Goliath*, but they are overcome. We're preparing to board *Goliath*. I ask that you stay below, out of harm's way."

"You said, 'All hands not otherwise engaged,'" the queen responded.

Inconstante's broadsides continued to fire but with less frequency. The barrage must have killed crew members and destroyed guns.

"Your Majesty," Lawford said, "unfortunately, I don't have time to debate this. I know you're a skilled swordswoman, but it's imperative that you stay safe. If we lose you, the crew will have sacrificed for no reason and the nation will have no ruler."

An unmistakable crack, like the felling of a large tree, reached them from across the water. Losing the mainmast would incapacitate *Inconstante*, leaving her unable to maneuver.

Queen Lenore said, "Captain, if you fail, there will be no escape. Every weapon matters. I will not hide below when I could lend my sword and inspire the crew."

Lawford could insist the queen remain, but while she did so, their opportunity to take *Goliath* dwindled. And the queen was right. Her presence would encourage the boarders and remind them they fought for more than their lives.

"Very well, but board only when the main deck has been cleared. Take no risks and stay with your detail." Lawford gave the queen's guards a stern look. "Do not leave her side. You know what's at stake."

Queen Lenore nodded and then joined the back of the nearest boarding party line.

Lawford turned to the helmswoman. "Cochrane, let's tap *Goliath* on the shoulder. Pass the word, silence on the ship now. Parker, prepare to sweep that deck and fire on my command."

Lawford made final preparations to collide with *Goliath*. Given the noise and chaos of battle, the smoke and fading light, it was too late when *Goliath*'s crew noticed HMS *Convert*'s approach. When the carronades were within range, Lawford yelled, "Fire!"

Grapeshot flew across *Goliath*'s deck. HMS *Convert* was in danger of a broadside salvo until the pirates were subdued, but they were occupied with firing on the other side of the ship. Cochrane guided HMS *Convert* to close the gap between the two ships. They came together with a rasping crash and crunch. The boarding crews immediately lashed the ships together and hauled planks for egress.

"On your command, Lieutenant Parker!"

Parker gave the order to charge, which was repeated down the line with great enthusiasm. She reached a plank with her musket drawn and dropped onto *Goliath*'s deck. Lawford left Cochrane in charge of the quarterdeck and crossed the plank to the pirate ship just in time to hear Parker call, "All clear on the main deck!"

The deck was clear in one sense. No pirate stood to challenge them, but grapeshot, splinters, broken rigging, and the dead were scattered about the deck. Smoke and the stench of blood and sulfur clung to everything. The pirates whose bodies remained had few proper weapons to repel boarders. Lough probably didn't want his men to have the means to challenge him. Daggers and other sharp objects lay among the bodies, but these would be no match for the muskets, pikes, and cutlasses carried by HMS *Convert*'s marines and crew.

Denholm and Lough were nowhere in sight, dead or alive. They would be waiting with the gun crews somewhere below deck.

Lawford heard fighting in the aft hold and followed the sounds, inspecting compartments for pirates as she went. The ship rocked with a loud crash. De Naumann and the Auvergnat would board soon.

As Lawford entered the aft hold, she shaded her eyes from the bright lantern light. As her eyes adjusted, she saw several marines standing around Parker as he oversaw the binding of the final pirate prisoners. Lawford slipped through the ring of marines. Queen Lenore stood on the other side with a look of triumph, flanked by her guards and holding two ornate swords. Denholm and Lough, both unconscious though apparently alive, were bound and lay not far from the queen's feet.

Lawford crossed to the queen's side and whispered, "Congratulations, Your Majesty. I'll look forward to hearing the details later, but the Auvergnat marines will board within minutes. With our countries at war, we must get you off this ship immediately."

Queen Lenore nodded and handed Lawford one of the two swords she was holding. "This is Lough's sword. It might come in handy when you negotiate."

"My thinking exactly. With your permission." Lawford nodded toward the other sword. "I believe you can keep your uncle's sword as a souvenir."

The queen smiled, indicated to her guards that they should follow her, and left the hold. Lawford ordered Parker to quietly evacuate the ship and prepare to shove off while she waited with the remaining marines and prisoners. Parker complied.

When Captain de Naumann and several armed officers entered the hold a few minutes later, Lawford wasn't sure what to expect. She greeted them warmly and thanked the captain for intervening to save HMS *Convert*. She explained the circumstances of the attack without mentioning the queen. Lawford offered the sword to de Naumann, "*Goliath*, the pirate prisoners, and Captain Lough's sword are yours."

The other captain refused the sword. "The prize is rightfully yours, according to international custom. You boarded first and struck the colors."

Lawford still did not withdraw the sword. "Without your assistance we would not have survived, and we do not have the resources or personnel to take the prize. We only wish to travel safely home."

De Naumann took the sword and offered her hand, which Lawford shook heartily.

WAR

THE CONFESSION

Written by Tim Grahl
Edited by Valerie Francis

Therapists have a big, four-dollar word for it. Countertransference.

When you wear the collar, it's just sin.

And it's true. It's obvious now, looking back. Long before this I had crossed a line, but at this moment there was no turning back.

I hadn't heard from Thomas in weeks. I knew in our last meeting he had hit a wall—a place in his mind he wasn't sure he wanted to go. I had reached out to him a couple of times to see if he wanted to meet so he could finish his confession, but there was no response.

This is where I should have let it lie. Even reaching out to him those times was beyond appropriate behavior. We are supposed to wait for the confessors to come. They have to be ready.

But I needed to know. How did this end?

I had spent several days down at the library searching the news reports, but they all spun the same narrative. A prison riot had turned into a standoff. In the end, it had turned deadly when the conspirators turned on each other.

This wasn't Thomas's story, though. He had been telling a much different tale.

I had to know the end.

In my line of work, I mostly see people at their lowest. They don't make a meeting with their priest because things are going well. It's when their spouses found the text messages or they had finally met up with the man in person or the company had gone bankrupt or the parents had found the drugs.

Or an old man facing down terminal cancer with a story that had been eating him alive for fifty years.

This is when I had to be a responsible priest. People at their lowest were afraid of eternal damnation and were looking to me for their path to salvation.

Only once in all of my years of shepherding did I truly take advantage of this situation, and that's how I got Thomas to see me one last time. When I dangled the choice between salvation and eternal damnation in front of the distraught, I figured they would do most anything.

At the time, I consoled my conscience with assurances that this was best for Thomas. He would be better once his confession was complete.

It's obvious now that did not turn out to be the case.

Thomas arrived at my office, and I could hear his cane tapping its way down the corridor. When I opened the door for him, he was agitated and downcast. He wouldn't make eye contact with me and turned down offers of refreshments.

"Let's get this over with," he said.

He took his chair, wincing on his way down. I took mine across from him and put on my most pious of faces to cover my own eagerness as he began.

. . . . . .

I watched as they dragged Alex's body to the back of the room. Carlos sifted through the heaps blocking the door until he found a cleanish mattress and dragged it back as well. Frank stepped forward to help him lift the young boy and placed him gently on the mattress. I got a look at his face right before the blanket covered it. Somehow he looked even younger than usual.

The forty or so men were still crowded around his body, many of them openly weeping.

I was still in shock myself. The young boy had been sent out to meet with them. To negotiate. He was the only one both sides had trusted. I knew what went on here wasn't any good, but I had no idea they would go as far as all-out murder.

But that's what they did. And I suppose I shouldn't have been surprised. I knew how Warden Lister worked. It's power—only and always power.

Lister returned the battered, broken body to the held-up inmates. It was a clear sign of what was to come.

One of the men—I can't place his name—spoke up at this point.

"Why did we do this? Is it really worth it? Look at him! He's the only truly innocent one of us and he's dead."

Frank stepped to the middle, almost as if protecting Alex's body.

"He is the reason we did this," he said, pointing at Alex's body. "No matter what goes on here and what they do to us, the truth is, this is where we all belong. We earned our spot here."

I was shocked to see tears welling up in Frank's eyes as he turned back to the boy. I didn't think anything but violence could ever emerge from his hulking frame.

"Not him, though. He had no place among us, yet he stood with us. He was the only truly righteous part of our struggle."

Silence fell over them as they all stared at the body, unsure of what to do next.

The radio by my side squawked to life at this somber moment and all eyes turned to me. I pushed myself back up, gasping against the pain in my leg.

Carlos came and stood over me.

"Answer it," he said.

I did. It wasn't the negotiator this time. It was Lister. He was only confirming what we all knew.

The reserves were coming. They were an hour out and they would be militarized. It wouldn't take long for them to organize and invade. Maybe thirty minutes. It would all be over in a couple of hours.

Carlos nodded, absently staring at the ground while chewing on his lip. All the other inmates waited for him to speak.

Several of the prisoners had turned themselves in after Alex's body was delivered.

"We all know what's coming," Carlos said. "We've seen the news report, how what we've done here has been twisted. To the outside world we're a bunch of savage rapists and killers. They haven't seen the beatings and tortures and every other way these monsters have fucked with us for years."

"And now we know they never will."

He motioned to Alex's body.

"They mean to kill us all. They can't let one of us stand at this point. Too much has happened. They're in too deep. They know we'll talk and talk and talk. Maybe nobody will believe us. But someone, somewhere will finally dig."

"This has to end clean for them, which means we all have to die."

"But some of you need to go."

Carlos stepped forward and clapped his hand on Emery's shoulder.

"You've got two little kids. They need their dad."

He locked eyes with another. I never got his real name, but they just called him Mongoose.

"And you've got a young wife who wants to see you again."

Carlos stepped back to address all of them.

"It's time for you to leave. Get out now. Turn yourselves in. Beg for forgiveness. Maybe you'll make it out of this intact."

Mongoose opened his mouth and started to argue, but Carlos waved his hand at him to cut him off.

Emery, Mongoose, and the others slowly moved past the barricade of doors and chairs and furniture that had been erected. God, had it only been two days ago? It seemed like this had gone on for ages.

I watched as Rand pulled back the door just enough to let the men move through. They each stuck out their hands first so the guards at the end of the hall could clearly see they were unarmed.

I was relieved when there weren't immediate gunshots. That's what I half expected. With everything that happened, and what we all knew was coming next, it wouldn't have surprised me if a trigger-happy guard lit into them at first sight.

I couldn't see from my spot on the floor, but I knew what was happening.

Each of them was being knocked to their knees and then laid down on their stomachs. Their wrists were zip-tied behind them. Extra tight. Then they were dragged to their feet and immediately led to either the D or E wings. Those were the smallest and most secure cells. They were also kept away from any public eyes. The debriefing would happen long before they were allowed to address anyone outside of the immediate system.

As Mongoose slipped past the barrier, Carlos appeared at my feet.

"How you feeling, boss?"

I pushed myself up against the wall and winced as I looked down at the wound.

They had cleaned me up the best they could, but there weren't any real medical supplies and the water had long since been cut off to this wing. I could see the blood seeping through the ripped-up sheet that had been tightly wound around my thigh.

They'd have to dig that slug out of my leg before a real autopsy was done on me. No sense having to explain why a bullet from a guard's gun ended up inside one of their compatriots.

"I'm okay. Hanging in there."

Carlos nodded.

"You ready to go then?"

"What do you mean?" I asked.

"This is it. You know what's coming next. You'll one hundred percent get caught in the crossfire. No reason for you to die here."

I studied Carlos's face for several seconds, but it was a block of stone as always.

"You know I can't go out there. They'd string me up for sure."

Carlos spat.

"Nah, you're one of their own. You get out there, get your story straight with theirs and you'll be fine. A dead guard riddled with bullets is something they'd rather avoid explaining I'm sure."

I shook my head.

"I can't do that. It's too late. I've seen too much. I know why you're here. Why you're doing this. I spent years telling myself the way we treated you was a necessity. It kept you in line. It kept you afraid, which is what we wanted. But now..."

I stopped and bit my lip. Carlos wasn't someone I was looking to cry in front of. I just shook my head again.

"I can't go back to the way things were. I deserve what you're going to get more than any of you."

Carlos nodded, satisfied with my response, and then he turned and called for the others to gather around. There were only a couple dozen left. The bodies of those who had been cut down in the clashes were covered and safe in the corners. The handful who surrendered were gone and the barrier was back in place.

"And why have you stayed? Why are we still here? That's the question that's been rolling around my head these past few hours. It's one thing to start something like this. We ain't the first riot in this place's history. Ain't the first standoff neither. But here we are."

"I suppose we could say we want to make a point, but we know that's not going to change anything. The world don't give a fuck about us. We're outta sight and outta mind. And Lister don't give a fuck neither."

Carlos paused and then let out a dark chuckle.

"I suppose he does now!"

There was a rowdy laugh at this. Rowdier than you would have thought, which I suppose was just the nervousness of everyone showing through.

"And since we're the prisoners and them the guards, them news trucks out there gonna be eating up every damn word they say and won't give a fuck why we done what we done. We'll just be the violent no-good criminals who don't know our place.

"So we can lay down and beg for mercy and see what happens. Or we can stay right here and stand against the shit they've been dumping on us for years. Some of us for decades. Stand up and say we're people just like they is people. We just made a few more mistakes. Don't mean we can be starved to death and beaten to death and coerced and shot and cut and used.

"Nobody else will know it, but we'll know it. As we go down, we'll know we stood for something. We stood for ourselves. And maybe, just maybe, when Lister and them guards have to look in the faces of those behind these bars, maybe they'll remember what's coming for them if things don't change."

Just then the radio at my side lit up again.

"Thomas? Thomas, you still with us?"

I glanced up at Carlos who took a step toward me at the noise. His eyebrows lifted questioningly.

"It's Lister," I said.

Carlos laughed. "He finally ready to give up?"

The men behind him laughed.

I picked up the radio, keeping eye contact with Carlos the whole time.

"Aye, still hanging on, sir."

"Good, good. We hope to see you soon."

I smiled at this.

"Tell Carlos and the others we can still end this peacefully. They come out, admit what they've done, and take their punishment like men. This doesn't have to end in blood."

Carlos snatched the radio out of my hand.

"You know, I think I will come out. I think that'd be best. My one demand is I get to see you face to face so I can rip your throat out and feed it to you other butt fuckers out there."

Carlos waited as the static of the radio hung.

"So that's a no?" Lister asked.

Another crack of loud laughter went through the men. I smiled at the knowledge that Lister could certainly hear the laughter from his station.

"I suppose so," Carlos responded and then turned and hurled the radio at the wall. Plastic and bits of electronics exploded and rattled to the floor.

He turned back to his men.

"I suppose we're committed here. Which is how it should be. I know some of you were with me on this plan from the beginning. Some of you just got caught up in the hysteria. But we all knew from the moment we threw that switch that this would be the end. There was no winning or getting out alive. Just this—us standing up for ourselves and our brothers here.

"We could have stayed in our cells, known our place, and had our souls snatched away from us or slowly rotted away. We ain't free out there, but we are free in here." Carlos beat his fist against his chest.

"But I could feel it slipping. You could feel it slipping. So now, as we get taken down by whatever goons they sending down from the Capitol. We can die happy. We can die with our souls intact."

At this, one of the men stepped forward. God help me if I can't remember his name either. But he was one of the younger ones. One of the ones who hadn't been there long enough to be broken. He should have stayed in his cell.

"Thank you," he said.

Carlos turned to him. "For?"

"All my life," the young man said, "all the men only hurt me. They beat me. Told me I was nothing. Told me I was worse than nothing. And I suppose they was right. Look where I ended up. And I was sent here for life. Nothing. That's what my life was. Just like my paps and my uncle had told me all them years."

He took a deep breath.

"But you gave me that back. Today I ain't nothing. You gave that to me. You wonder why we stayed with you? I could have stayed in my cell and died a nothing in forty, fifty years. Or I could stand with you and die now as something. That's a gift, man. That's something no one else ever gave me a chance at."

Several men were nodding along with him when Frank limped forward and cleared his throat.

His calf was wrapped up like mine with a bullet still stuck in there, yet he was walking on it. He was covered with scrapes and bruises. The gash along his forearm was starting to streak with red from the infection. He had made plenty of the guards pay for their intrusion on our territory.

I don't know if anyone had ever heard him speak. I know I hadn't, in the decade of time I'd been haunting those halls, and he had been there long before me.

But he spoke now.

"I've been here a very long time. Longer than any of you. I thought I was the strongest and the toughest around. Most of the guards didn't much mess with me.

"When I first heard what Carlos was planning, I thought it was silly. Stupid. I'd seen what they'd done to Charlie. Hell, they had me help take what was left of his body up to the morgue. And there'd been plenty of Charlies before. I had always seen them as weak. Unable to survive this jungle like I did.

"But then I seen it for what it was. We ain't animals. This ain't a jungle. We are people. Humans. We done wrong, sure. We bought our tickets to this hellhole, but that don't change what we are. That don't change what's in our souls.

"I was planning on growing old in this place. I'd figured it out. I'd make it and eventually die a peaceful death one night in my sleep. Maybe even with one of those pretty nurses upstairs watching over me. But then that son of a bitch over there," he motioned to Carlos, "made me see what was really going on. And once you wake up, you can't just go back to sleep. Can you?

"So here in a bit we are gonna fight. And we are gonna die. But I'd rather go out standing up as a human and a man than die as a broken-down survivor."

I don't know why I did it. Up till now I had said as little as possible. I still represented the enemy among these men, after all. I still had the blues and the badge, as they say.

But I'd seen too much to stay silent.

"I'd like to say something, if that's okay."

I searched the faces of Carlos and Frank and the other men, but it was obvious any hatred they had for me had leaked away now that I was facing their same fate.

"I'm the reason you're here. I'm the reason it came to this. I can blame Lister and my superiors, but men like me did what we were told for the last ten years. We didn't question. We just pushed those voices in our heads that were telling us this was all so wrong and just shoved that shit down and did our jobs."

Tears started welling in my eyes again, but I didn't stop them this time.

"So I'm sorry. To each of you. I'm sorry to your families. I'm sorry to those who love you. I'm sorry I pushed you to this place where you finally had to stand up. Cause it ain't what you deserved.

"I'm going to die with you today because I don't think I can live out there anymore. I'd have to carry around each of your deaths." My eyes cut to the corner where the bodies were laid out. "Alex's especially. And I don't think that's a weight my soul can carry.

"I did awful, evil things here. I felt it was my job, my duty. But I was wrong. Some wrongs can be forgiven, but others can't. So today I'll die for my sins just as I should."

As I finished, a quiet hung over the group, and we heard a rumble from outside. One of the men at the edge of the group hopped up and looked out the window.

"They're here," he said.

"Alright," Carlos said. He crossed himself quickly. "Now's the time to get right with Jesus cause you gonna see him soon."

· · · · · ·

Quiet hung between Thomas and me. I wasn't sure what to say.

Up until now he had remained stoic through the entire story, but now he began to sob. His back heaved, and tears dripped to the floor.

He went on for several minutes. I let him get it all out. In a way, I was relieved.

"I'm not sure why you came to me to be absolved," I said. "It seems you stood for the right thing. Obviously, you got out, but you don't have to die to make it right."

Thomas rubbed hard at his eyes, wiping away the last of the tears. He lifted his cane, planted it hard on the floor, and forced himself up to his feet.

"You don't get it," he said. "There's a reason I didn't come back to tell you the end. Because I realized I can't ever be forgiven for what I did."

"Thomas, God can forgive any—"

He waved his hand to cut me off.

"You know what I've been living on these last twenty years since I retired?"

I stared blankly at him.

He smiled sadly at me.

"My government pension. It's a good one too. I was the only one who made it out of that room alive. Then the day after they released me from the hospital, I reported back to the jail for duty and worked under Lister until we both retired the same year.

"I watched those men die. I made promises to them. I made promises to myself. But when push came to shove—when it was time to make a stand—I just went back to work. Kept the same system going. Participated too.

"So tell me, preacher, how many Hail Marys I gotta do to skip out on hell now?"

I didn't answer as he turned to the door and started tapping his way back down the hallway. I didn't have to. We both knew the truth.

Hell was the only place good enough for him.

HORROR

OUTPOST 5

Written by J. Thorn
Edited by Ira Heinichen

No. Not days, weeks, or months. Years. If you'd been the sentry at Outpost 5, alone and left with nothing but that incessant, howling wind, you'd have done the same thing.

Of course, I knew Articles 1 and 2 of the Sentry Code of Conduct.

Never leave the outpost.

Never kill.

But you weren't there. You didn't have the alpha male in your head. You didn't see the hellfire in that boy's eyes. Let me explain...

Howling. A figment of my imagination, I thought. It had been so long since I'd seen anything.

I remember looking up and seeing that full moon glaring down upon me—a cold, silver eye of judgment. It was as if the moon knew, like it sent those creatures to test me. They came from the darkness, sentient and unforgiving.

The wolves crept through the ruins, down asphalt streets cracked by time, and through the burnt-out hulls of automobiles from another age. At first, I'd only seen seven or eight—all following the alpha male. He led the pack, dark fur greasy and matted, eyes as piercing as the moon's glare. I could taste a musty odor on my tongue when the wind changed and pushed their scent to me.

I checked my journal. One hundred and eighty days. That's how long it had been since I'd seen another living creature, not counting the rats I'd trapped in the ruins. Those foul things were nothing but sustenance, no different than the bland weeds I'd used to make soup or the labelless canned goods I'd scavenged.

The last animal to pass my outpost was a dog—a black Labrador retriever with fur so dark it swallowed the night. I had let the dog go. I was a grown man before the bombs fell. I remembered what it was like to walk a dog, to play fetch, to have one curled up at my feet on a cold winter morning.

The wolves, they were another story. Yes, I understand dogs evolved from them. But not these wolves. The ones that approached my outpost had been born and bred of the apocalypse—desperate, hungry, a band of hunters no longer resembling anything close to our domesticated friends.

I'd read the manual every week, if for no other reason than to occupy my mind. I had even memorized the first seven articles of the Code of Conduct. What else was there to do on those cold, lonely, eternal nights?

Like an obedient sentry, I raised my rifle and fired over the heads of the three wolves closest to me—warning them to keep away from Outpost 5. Article 2 says that life can only be taken in defense of one's own and I could not yet justify an act of self-defense.

While the trio of gunshots echoed through the vast, steel canyons, the alpha male stopped and stared at me—as if daring me to put the crosshairs on him.

Maybe his spell worked, or maybe I had simply decided to spare them all. Regardless, I left the alpha male standing. That was the night's first complication, but not the one that shook me to my core. No, that happened when a boy emerged from a pile of rubble, a building that had once been a supermarket. He moved amongst the wolves almost as if one of them.

He said nothing, simply walked toward me with his eyes locked on mine. Yes, I had been as shocked as you are now to discover that other humans had been living in the ruins, practically at my feet.

I watched as the boy approached, hunched over and shuffling from one burnt-out car to another. He stopped and stared at me, his hands behind his back.

"Identify yourself." Protocol. I followed it and asked for his name.

He shook his head, his eyes darting back and forth beneath shaggy bangs. Now he walked in a straight line—right at me.

"Killing violates the second article of the Code of Conduct. But I can defend myself." This sounded odd in my ears, as if I had somehow been rationalizing my own defense. At the least, I would shoot and maim him. Of that, I had no doubt.

The boy stopped not more than ten feet from my position. I could smell his rank body and hear him wheezing. And then he grinned at me, his teeth black as pitch.

"Save him."

At first, I thought the boy had spoken those words about the alpha male.

"You must save him."

But the child's lips had not moved. I turned to glance through the scope at the alpha male when the voice filled my ears again.

Was it in my ears or in my head? I didn't know. It had been 310 days since I last had a conversation, but I was still a rational person. I knew when a voice was in my head and when it was coming from somewhere else.

And as sure as I sit here speaking with you, I had done so with the wolf. Many things in this universe remain a mystery to me, but I'm not insane. As I talk to you, so the alpha male did with me.

"Why?" I asked. My throat felt raw, my tongue clumsy as the sound of my own voice rattled inside of my skull.

"He's a savage without empathy. You must do something for the child."

The alpha male sat on its haunches while the other wolves gathered behind him, all of them sitting upon the top floor of a second-story building that had once been a coffee house. Clouds slithered by that celestial, evil eye, puncturing a hole through a black velvet sky.

"Abandoning my post and taking him back to the settlement is against Article 3 of the Code of Conduct."

"Are you not pledged to prioritize human life?" The alpha male's ears twitched. "You have a responsibility to more than just Article 3."

I looked back at the boy. He now stood before me, beneath a traffic light dangling from a sagging wire. The boy had extended his arms, standing in a Jesus Christ pose as the wolf continued to speak.

"He's a child. And he's a human. This world may be cursed, evil. But the children are not."

I'd been staring at the wolf through my scope when I saw a flicker in its eyes. The others behind the alpha male leaped to their feet.

"Look!"

I turned around in time to see the boy coming at me. His face was frozen inside of a plastic-edged portrait, as if I'd taken a picture of him with the technology of a lost age—the image now burned into my memory.

The boy looked at me through bloodshot eyes, empty as if this world shattered the soul behind them. Blood and scars covered his dirt-encrusted face, his lips snarled into a grimace. His hair smelled like a stable full of soiled straw, and I could hear his lungs rattling, no doubt from years of breathing the toxic dust without a mask.

He held a knife in his right hand, the tip of it aimed at my heart.

The alpha male howled, as confused by the boy's attack as I was. The poor kid had lost all sense of his humanity and was nothing more than a savage beast in the barren wasteland.

I spun to the side, lifting my rifle to block his attack. Ducking down, I swept his legs out from underneath him with my right foot and then planted my left on his chest, pinning him to the ground. He screamed, a sound that raised the hairs on the back of my neck. The boy's arms and legs spasmed like an insect pinned to a board—alive.

When I looked back to the alpha male, I noticed he'd come down off the building and was now slowly walking toward me. His eyes darted back and forth as some of the pack began to whine.

"Take no life," the wolf said. "Those at the settlement can save him."

Yes, even then, I understood the ramifications of my actions. I'd taken counsel from a monster and had subdued a child. I had not forsaken my responsibilities, but if the boy could not be tamed I'd certainly bend the Code backward like a palm tree in a hurricane.

The threat must be eliminated.

I'd remembered that saying during my weeks of training all those years ago.

We'd lost billions of people; 99 percent of the population gone. We couldn't afford to add more casualties to that holocaust, and I had been trained to preserve life at all costs. But this child had intended to murder me, and if he had succeeded, there would have been nobody to man Outpost 5—to protect all of you in the settlement. I would have accepted my punishment for breaking Article 2 if it meant bringing a child back to the settlement. But this wasn't a normal boy.

I swung the rifle around and put the barrel against the boy's forehead. "Don't move or I'll put a bullet in your brain. Do you understand?"

He didn't move. The boy said nothing, but I could see the answer in his eyes. He understood.

"You must honor Article 1. Lower your weapon," said the alpha male, now twenty yards to my right and at the base of a twenty-foot oak that had sprouted and grown through a mailbox on the corner of Main Street and 5th.

I slung the rifle over my shoulder until it rested on my back. Reaching to my belt, I grabbed two zip ties—using one to secure the boy's wrists and the other on his ankles. I knew it would hold. Not even decades of toxic fallout could weaken the zip ties. Our plastic would outlast the cockroaches.

When I was a child, my father had locked me in my bedroom, tied to a chair. From the time I was five years old, he'd do this every week. He'd told me he was "making me a man," and that someday I'd be grateful for his tough love. He was right. Had he not taught me how to endure pain, I would have never survived the apocalypse.

And so, I did the same for this boy. I saw the lessons of my childhood reflected in his eyes. If I were to eventually bring the child back to the settlement, he'd need to be strengthened—forged in the flame of pain as I had been.

I felt a flutter in my chest, and a smile broke across my wind-burned face as I stood over the boy. His terror fueled my righteousness. I was teaching this feral beast how to be a human—a man. It was nothing more than that.

"We can help you," said the alpha male, interrupting my thoughts.

"How?"

"Your code prevents you from harming the boy."

"No. From killing him," I said.

"You have looked into his eyes. You know he cannot be reasoned with. Do you not?"

It felt as though the ground beneath my feet had begun to give way. I'd felt this before when exploring the ruins, like stepping upon a slab of crumbling concrete that would slide into a sinkhole.

But both of my feet were firmly planted in the dirt, one on each side of the boy who was still on his back and bound by the zip ties.

"You're trying to trick me."

"No," said the alpha male. "This arrangement would be of mutual benefit. We can watch the boy while you sleep—on the journey back to the settlement."

The wolf's words had begun to soften my stance. I could feel the creature's influence burrowing into my brain, making me question my own judgment and training. This predator of the ruins was manipulating me, but I was doing my best to resist.

"We want to help."

"Why?" I asked.

"We raised him. The boy belongs to our clan, but he needs contact with his own. If his sickness is not dealt with soon, his poison will infect you before spreading to your clan, wherever they might be hiding."

I began to feel nauseated, each word from the alpha male turning my stomach like sour milk. That clever beast had showed his hand. I quickly realized he didn't know the location of the settlement and he hoped to use the boy to find it. I could not let that happen.

But the alpha male continued to worm into my brain. I had no way of knowing how long I could fight the creature's mental powers. I tried to think about all of my options, but a fog had filled my head. The wolves had come closer.

"No. You want to use my responsibility to the boy so you can find the settlement. I'm a Sentry of the Realm. My sworn duty is to guard Outpost 5 and keep the location of our settlement secure and—"

I stopped reciting the Code when I saw more wolves crawling from the ruins like an oil slick. They approached soundlessly, surrounding their leader and with all eyes on me.

"Don't."

Now, I felt more than just the alpha male in my head. Other word fragments and thoughts of delicious violence flooded my mind. I could not let them trick me.

"Don't hurt the child."

I would be forced to break the Code to uphold it, a sacrifice of one for many—irreconcilable goods. If you'd never spent time at an outpost, you'd never understand this paradox. But I did.

"Remember the Code."

I swung my rifle around, switched off the safety, put the barrel on the boy's forehead, and pulled the trigger. One, sharp crack reverberated through the empty city as I inhaled the reek of gunpowder and burnt flesh.

The boy was dead. A single, unblinking, red eye above his other two. And I had failed.

Almost immediately, the alpha male spun and turned to saunter back into the ruins from which he had come. The dozens of wolves that had gathered at his feet also turned, following their leader.

The alpha male would not be able to use the boy to find our settlement. I'd made sure of that. A single bullet secured our future.

You're welcome.

The voices inside my head disappeared, leaving no trace. Within moments, I'd been left alone at Outpost 5 as I'd been for the previous 311 days. Except now, I would have to dig a shallow grave before returning to the settlement. I'd failed to uphold the Code of Conduct, but I would own my failure and report it to you. Article 7 says that all deaths must be reported. I struggled as I left Outpost 5, my sworn duty. But I couldn't live with that child's blood on my hands—the shame and the guilt eating away at me.

And so, here we are. You are questioning me, as you should. As I would do if another sentry had abandoned his outpost and returned to the settlement.

But you should have seen me. You should have seen how wisely I proceeded—with what caution—with what foresight, with what dissimulation I covered my tracks!

I think you can also see that I saved the boy's soul. I prevented the alpha male from damning him for all eternity. And I saved us because the wolves could not follow the boy back to the settlement. He would have found it. The child had found Outpost 5.

Howling? No, I did not hear anything. It must be a figment of your imagination.

CRIME

LET JUSTICE PREVAIL

Written by Mark McGinn
Edited by Leslie Watts

Detective Sam Currie returned from the bar called The Alibi with the team's commiseration drinks. She forced a smile at her boss, Detective Sergeant Lee Anstiss, but his smacked-ass face since the verdict thirty minutes earlier was now set in concrete. She placed his beer and two double Bombay and tonics on the round table—one for her and one for their colleague, Detective Toni Tuck. The place was a regular cop hangout where court staff and defense lawyers, those brave enough, would assemble from 1600 hours and swap legal war stories. For the moment it was still quiet.

Without thanks, Lee Anstiss downed half his beer in one open-throat swallow, banged the glass on the table and declared he needed to take a piss.

Currie said, "Did you get your bladder from Costco?"

Anstiss, in no mood for humor, left for the urinal without a word, his shoulders slumped in defeat. He seemed to have disregarded the prosecutor's pretrial advice that the verdict could go either way.

Currie watched Tuck apply lip moisturizer with the skill of Georgia O'Keeffe. "Love this gin," she said, "but it's death to these babies, especially in bloody winter." Finished, she dropped the tube into her purse with the subtlety of a B-45 Tornado, sipped the gin and left her wet smudge of DNA over the glass. "Fuckin' juries, eh," she said with a head shake.

Currie said, "This one seems to have tortured him more than normal."

"None of us can be surprised, though, not if we're honest. No dead body is a hard sell."

Currie nodded. "Hard to speak for her when we haven't found her. Thing is, who else could have made her disappear? The way she doted on that little dog and the way Taylor couldn't stand it? There's no way she'd have abandoned it to him."

They'd looked at workmates and other family. No one else but Eddie came within a bull's roar of being a suspect.

Anstiss returned, tension still in his shoulders, the tired and sagging profile of a colleague Currie had worked with for ten years. He stared at his half-drunk beer, took a deep breath and sighed.

"We win most, Lee," Currie said, tone placatory. "Our hit rate with juries is decent when you think about it, especially yours."

He nodded, seemingly more in acknowledgment than in agreement. He started to repeat the prosecutor's speech. No one else had a motivation to kill Colleen Taylor. Much loved by friends, her hospo workmates, liked by neighbors. What woman just disappears off the face of the earth with no one hearing from her for a year, no passport ever issued in her name? It had to be the husband, Eddie.

Tuck looked at Currie, raised her dark eyebrows, and Currie mirrored the gesture. They could repeat all of this in their sleep.

When Anstiss took a sip of his beer, Currie interjected. "The whole murder squad agrees with you, Lee. And the stats tell us 90 percent of perps are within or closely connected to the family."

"Didn't help," he said, "when the bloody judge excluded our evidence on that data."

Tuck said, "Arresting him on the anniversary of her workmates reporting Colleen's disappearance probably didn't help us much either."

Lee glared at her. They knew that was his call. He thought it added to the poignancy of the situation, gave them an edge in the media that would reignite the fading story. Currie knew Tuck was trying to keep the conversation away from what happened to Colleen's parents after the not guilty verdict and Lee's appalling reaction. Both mother and father were so distressed with the verdict they needed medical attention. And Lee's reaction? "You don't know how I feel." It was a thoughtless response to the attending medics and they all knew it. It was as if he wasn't aware of what he was saying, a dramatic end to a very sad day. Only Eddie Taylor and his new girlfriend, the one who moved in with him two weeks after Colleen went missing, were happy. But as Currie massaged her right temple, she knew something wasn't right, something her mind refused her access.

Tuck asked, "Why didn't we give any evidence about Colleen Taylor's false burglary claim?"

Anstiss said, "Eddie put her up to it, but the problem was, that would've been harder to prove than proving he murdered her. I wanted the prosecutor to use it as a motive for Eddie to kill her— that she fucked up the burglary story, compromised him, and in a rage, he killed and got rid of her. But she said we needed more evidence. The new girlfriend was a better motive because there was plenty of evidence there. I guess that made sense in the end."

"When did you decide to drop the fraud charges against her?" Tuck asked.

"When we hadn't found her after six months."

Currie frowned. There was something wrong here. The timing. It had to be in the timing. The complaint from the insurance company was made to police before Colleen went missing. Had Anstiss sat on that? Had he been distracted by a relationship breakdown or too busy with other cases?

"And I never understood why the defense made a big issue about that photo of the boy," Tuck said.

"Don't you two turn into defense counsel," Anstiss said. "I've had a gut full of all the so-called unanswered questions about why she staged a burglary and where the photo disappeared to. You realize no one apart from Ted McKee ever claims to have seen that photo? No one." Currie heard resentment in his tone. He added, "Ted confused himself with another case. Needs to be put out to pasture."

Currie and Tuck looked away from him. The defense made too much of those issues, created a heavy smokescreen. They said it pointed to an untidy investigation, sloppy even, and that was a huge red flag when they were already struggling without a body.

Currie resolved to return to the squad room but decided not to tell Lee. Nothing she did from here would change the verdict but applying a fresh lens other than on Eddie Taylor's guilt might help gain new insight into where Colleen's body might be. They all had their roles in the team, but body recovery hadn't been her role. That was Tuck's, under Lee's direction. For now, he wasn't in the mood to hear anything other than Eddie Taylor was a murderer wandering the streets and that the jury were a pack of ignoramuses.

After switching to nonalcoholic drinks, she drove Tuck and Anstiss to their homes, neither of them fit to drive. Anstiss couldn't have driven, even if he was sober. He'd told them about the repeated failure of the USB port in his Honda, so it was in the auto electrician's workshop. Currie switched off during Anstiss's second rendition, unable to let go of the idea that there was a connection to be made between insurance, the photo of a boy, and where the body might be.

Back at work, Currie's gut wrench returned. It was a familiar feeling, an intrusion whenever she thought about Anstiss swearing her to secrecy about separating from his partner before they knew Colleen was missing. The pact allowed him to continue to work the Taylor investigation. "I need the distraction," he'd said. "You guys are my best mates, my support network."

Now, she wondered if keeping his secret had contributed to Taylor's acquittal. Had Lee really been up to leading a murder inquiry? She'd had her own "time out" to lick emotional wounds when she and her partner of five years drifted apart and finally separated. She should've insisted Lee do the same.

Back at her desk, she pored over the case file photos and listened to the taped interview with Colleen's parents and other witnesses. But she was coming up short on any new lead on where Colleen might be buried—something to help them all feel different about the lack of justice.

By the time police interviewed Taylor, he'd had a year to get his story straight. The investigation into him as a possible suspect responsible for her death and disappearance was prompted by Colleen's workmates. They'd become suspicious about Eddie's lack of concern about his missing wife. He would only say Colleen told him she was leaving him for good. She didn't take her belongings because the commune gave her a list of what she was allowed. Currie knew the commune story was a ruse. They all did.

And when she'd been gone two weeks, Eddie Taylor took all her clothing to the tip. But he couldn't account for why her credit card had been used only for purchasing liquor when she'd never drunk an alcoholic drink in her life and had no prior history of liquor purchases before she disappeared. The team presented this detail in court, presented Taylor as having made a mistake—that at some point his wife would've told her friends she didn't drink. But they couldn't prove the identity of the person using the card and the defense argued the liquor could've been mail order on an unknown device to an unknown address. Taylor said the commune would've confiscated her credit card and devices. It was rabbit hole evidence.

Taylor's computer showed search histories for investigations involving missing persons, several months before Colleen's friends became suspicious. In one search, Taylor typed, *Best techniques for burying a body.* When confronted with his search histories, Taylor admitted them with glee. He'd published six crime stories on Amazon. He offered to sign a printed title for Anstiss. Currie thought that was a convenient line, something into which Lee could've been more probing if he'd been more on his game. He let it form part of the case against Eddie, but they had nothing on rebuttal.

Currie dug out the complaint from the insurance company. The alleged stolen items: assorted jewelry, a camera, a computer, a Bose sound system. Photos and receipts were provided, and the claim was dated six weeks before she failed to attend work at the *At Rest Hotel.* The insurance company's PI said the so-called stolen items had been hidden in her own garage cupboards.

Currie returned to the murder file. The statements of witnesses and financial records were enough to get a search warrant of the Taylor house and vehicles. Amongst the property taken in the search were the items she'd claimed were stolen as well as a sled on wheels they'd all believed once helped transport Colleen's body. It had her DNA on the boards but what did that mean? Anstiss thought Eddie used it to transport her body to a burial site. But it didn't have Eddie's DNA on it.

Then the photo, also listed in the inventory. Eddie claimed he hadn't seen it before the search. As an afterthought, he speculated Colleen had brought it home from work. He couldn't or wouldn't identify who was in the pic. Ted McKee's search record said "loose photo found in Colleen Taylor's diary: suited man with young boy, *At Rest Hotel.*"

Currie, leaning back in her chair, stared at the fly shit on the ceiling and then checked the work roster. Close to midnight, the death watch shift would be taking their break. McKee was on. She took the stairs to the level below, found him in his pigpen, feet on the desk, reading Milton Helpern's *Autopsy.*

"Learning anything?" she asked.

He looked up at the clock above the door. "Can't you keep away, Currie? You get no thanks, you know."

"I know. Something I can't let go of. Trying to help Colleen Taylor's parents recover her body."

"Know what that's like. What can I do?"

She went over the facts and he looked at the handwritten inventory document, confirmed it was his own writing.

She asked, "What did Anstiss say about it when the pic couldn't be found back here?"

"I thought he was gonna kick my ass. But he said it wasn't a big deal, wasn't relevant to the murder investigation."

"We keep all sorts of material that might not seem relevant. Right? What's unknown today might be known tomorrow."

"I agree. But he had a huge hard-on for Eddie Taylor. Nothing else seemed to matter."

"Was there anything you remember about the boy in the picture?"

He nodded and looked sad. "His little tortured face looking behind, probably turned to the lens when the elevator's bell sounded. Reckon he'd have been no more than twelve or thirteen years old."

"And the man?"

He shook his head. "Boy came up to the guy's hip. A suit, facing away from the camera, holding the boy's hand."

Back at her desk, Currie texted Anstiss. *Pik u up in the am.* She drove home, deciding also to pick up Tuck in the morning after Lee. Tuck could continue to play the naïve inquirer and cajole him into painful reflections he'd been avoiding. It wouldn't matter if Anstiss spotted it. Currie could still be "the good cop." She needed him to see that the only way he could move forward, let this case go without it eating him alive, was to admit he played a part in creating reasonable doubt. Despite the statistical odds in his favor, he'd put Eddie Taylor in the cross hairs too soon. And she was his accomplice to him not being fit for purpose. If she could admit her part because of their past relationship, it might help him.

In the morning there was a decent snow dump. A heated and chauffeured drive would hopefully put him in a better mood for more questions. Driving to his Somerfield apartment, her mind drifted to why Chrissy Anstiss walked out on Lee. He never said that day on their bike ride in Burwood Forest. Was it the same reason as her partner left her? Time poor, conflicting work patterns, low intimacy—these were relationship killers. Male cops initiated comfort sex with grateful but vulnerable victims of crime. Or, cooped up on investigation with each other for a long period of time, cops would go at it. But their partners seldom uncovered it. Had he been caught out?

Her idea was to slowly ease into the part he played in the case going pear-shaped. She'd do it gently. It wouldn't matter if he broke down, as he did when he told her about Chrissy. He needed a catharsis, not an impenetrable suit of armor. She speed-dialed Tuck to talk over her plan. The call went straight to Tuck's voicemail.

Currie turned into Anstiss's street and saw his blue Accord speed away from his driveway. She accelerated, following a discreet distance behind. Surely, he couldn't have got it back last night. And didn't he get her text?

If he was heading to work, he could've taken any one of three right turns to do so. Instinct told her to keep following. Moving away from a set of lights, she let a car get between them. At the green, it was clear he wasn't going into work. Did he lie about the broken USB port? Twice? In ten minutes Anstiss was in Eddie Taylor's street. Currie pulled up behind a tree in the leafy avenue, almost completely out of sight. Anstiss got out, checked up and down the street, and jogged to Taylor's front porch, leaving his car unlocked. In time, he emerged with Taylor dressed in black cycling Lycra. The Honda took off at speed, increasing the distance between them and away from their police station.

After twenty minutes of heading east and some deft manipulation to be second car behind Anstiss, Currie was eventually forced to give way to traffic with a green arrow right of way. Anstiss had gone through the intersection, late on orange. She banged the steering wheel and cursed the seconds of delay and the truck and trailer that now completely blocked her view.

Lee's new pursuit of Eddie Taylor meant there was no way she could involve Tuck who was now too far away. Priorities had changed. Currie realized heading east in this part of town meant Lee had somehow turned Taylor. This drive, in this direction, meant finding the body. It had to.

They headed toward Plantation Road in Burwood. That made sense. The forest was acres of pine, a labyrinth of walking and biking tracks. It was the place she and Lee had ridden together, a place from which you exited by compass. He took her to what he said was the best way in. She went that way now and thought about calling it in to give directions. But it was clear he wanted no fanfare. A quiet triumph was all he needed. He hadn't lied about not having his car. In his emotional distress over the verdict, he'd simply been overwrought and confused. Now, Lee Anstiss deserved her respect and she'd give it. She risked speeding to catch up, intent on quietly videoing the moment for Lee on her phone.

In ten minutes, she was in the forest, still on the snow-covered road with rows of pines all around her. Dappled light and shadow made it difficult to get good vision beyond the first couple of tree rows. And if she was right, Lee and Taylor would be off the beaten track now.

At a parking bay, his Honda was the solitary vehicle. No other sensible person would be walking or biking in these frigid conditions. This was a breakthrough they'd all wanted. Colleen's body would help them all move on. Lee had built something with Eddie Taylor, gotten him to talk. She'd underestimated her colleague. Worse, she'd come to think he wasn't up to the job. She'd projected how she felt about her own divorce on to him. The only viable forensics would be in the grave. Let him emerge triumphant, show the jury, the news media, the whole community that he'd been right to charge Eddie Taylor with murder even if Taylor got away with it. Lee deserved that vindication. The system had let him down. You win some, lose some. It was a numbers game.

Rain this side of town had washed away a lot of the snow. Out of the warmth of her car, she spotted bike tire tracks. The fanatics were out. And footprints. What would Taylor's directional instinct have been that dreadful day? On or off track. Off. He wouldn't want to be disturbed or seen by others. And even if he had used the four-wheeled sled, Taylor would've instinctively looked for flat ground. This sharpened her focus. She'd lost another minute before she picked up two sets of prints, one behind the other at arm's length. A long, Lee Anstiss arm length. She jogged where the prints took her and came to a clearing.

Currie saw Anstiss before he saw her. He was side on to her, but she could see he was looking upward. She was momentarily confused by his smile. Surely he would be looking down. Graves were down, not up. No longer jogging, but walking at pace, her eye followed his gaze. Taylor wriggled and jerked in the forlorn hope he might free himself from the tight noose around his neck. The other end of the rope wound around a horizontal bough the size of Currie's leg.

NO! Before Lee saw her, she had her weapon in hand.

"Back off, Lee," Currie yelled, sighting the barrel of her Glock on his upper body before he realized she was there. "Back off, now." Her voice bounced around the silent forest.

"Get out of here, Currie. Let justice prevail." He reached inside his jacket with his right hand.

Currie fired a warning shot and ran closer. Anstiss dropped his hands. "You're too late," he said with a rictus smile. She could swivel the gun sight to the rope but if she did, Lee's gun would be on her by the time she fired. She could miss the rope and lose her life. "Sorry, Lee," she said lowering her weapon. She fired, his right knee collapsed and he dropped to the ground, the shock on his face palpable. He reached again for his Glock. Currie put a bullet in his right shoulder. It gave her time to fire three shots at the rope. The third let Taylor's body fall to the soft snow beneath him.

Anstiss said, "Finish me off, Sam. Don't let this run on. Put my gun in my hand. You'll have self-defense."

The same ambulance took them both, an armed uniform cop between them.

Currie saw them the next day, Taylor first, in a different ward. Taylor told her he went with the detective because he'd been asked to identify Colleen's body. Anstiss had said there were no consequences for him doing so, but he needed a positive ID of some things in the grave before he approached Colleen's parents.

"Anstiss looked more relieved than angry, hopeful, even," Taylor said. "He was a different man."

The site Anstiss chose to kill Eddie Taylor proved to be the same site Lee Anstiss buried Colleen Taylor.

From Lee's bedside, he said, "Eventually, when Taylor's body was discovered, it would be assumed guilt finally got the better of him."

"It was the insurance claim. Wasn't it?" Currie asked.

"I confronted Colleen after the complaint from the insurance company." He looked away. "She provided me with the boy, a nephew. And then she got greedy. She wanted more than the money for him. Somehow, she took photos of me with him, blackmail. Then, Ted McKee got to her diary before I did. I thought it was one of the things Eddie had gotten rid of when I first turned over their place. When McKee and I were there together with the warrant. I got rid of the photo but he'd already made the inventory record."

Anstiss started to weep. "She told me the fake burglary paled against what she had on me. She started wanting big money from me, Sam. I had no fucking idea what to do except that I couldn't let it go."

Currie stood.

"Don't go, Sam. Please. Stay with me."

"Chrissy found out?"

He shook his head. "She left before Colleen and Eddie Taylor fucked up my life. She suspected. I don't know how. I was always discreet."

"And the boy? What about him?"

"I wasn't his first. Caught him attempting to break into a car, belonging to a prominent businessman. He asked me to bring him the boy, said he wouldn't press charges. When it was my turn, I wasn't rough with him. And if it wasn't me, it would've been someone else."

"This prominent businessman—what do we know about him?"

Anstiss moved his head on the pillow, small side-to-side movements. "Saving that, Sam. Might be worth something off my minimum parole period."

"What's happened to the boy?"

"Like I said, he'll have other happy, high-paying clients. He won't talk. Good money at stake. He gets whatever he wants, whenever he wants it. That's what he's thinking."

"You used her criminality to sexually abuse a child and when it backfired you murdered her. What's the autopsy going to tell us?"

"Strangulation." He wiped his eyes using the shoulder that still worked. "You should've finished me off."

"If I'd known, I might have. Now, everyone gets the justice they deserve and we both know yours won't be pretty."

THRILLER

X PASS

Written by Rebekah Olson
Edited by Randall Surles

The rented minivan inched between the traffic lights through downtown. Zach fidgeted in the passenger seat. He could walk faster than this. So close to getting the sweet justice the courts denied him and gridlocked traffic held him up. He clenched his teeth. The driver was doing well, patiently navigating the gridlock, which was better than drawing unnecessary attention. So close. If he didn't need the five guys in the back of the van, he'd jump out and run.

"Are you sure about this?" his friend asked, squished between two of the larger men in the back. He must be having doubts again. The guy was decent enough, had proved useful in tight situations, but he had a yellow streak as long as an arctic winter night.

"You're the one who told me," Zach reminded him. "Or were you making it up?"

"No, no. I wasn't making up anything."

"So she really does come have lunch with her jerk dad every Friday? She really does bring my kid with her?" Zach leaned to see his friend better, eyes narrowed. If they had gone to all this trouble and risk for nothing... He clenched his fist. "You weren't just saying that to make me happy. Were you?"

"They'll be there. But... if we're caught, I'm as good as fired."

"You hate that job," Zach said with a shrug. "Retail jobs are for wussies anyway. What kind of man wants to work in a downtown mall? Or do you like going shopping in all the other little stores in the building after they decide to let you off your chain?"

Some of the others snickered. His friend hunched his head down like a turtle and said, "I still think we shouldn't all go in at once."

"It'll be fine." Zach waved that away and turned to face the front. He squeezed the door handle, itching to open it and jump out. "Once we get the chaos going, they'll be so busy they might not even notice you. So you can keep your girlie job after all."

Finally, the minivan crossed the last intersection. The driver stopped at the curb where the glass face of one of the mall's entrances stood open in welcome. Zach jumped out and threw open the slider door for the others. "Let's roll."

"What the..." Jane frowned at the security monitor. "Lysle, did you see that?"

"Uh..." Lysle looked up from his college textbook. "What?"

"Just because I'm nice doesn't mean you get to stop paying attention!"

"I'm studying for that test." He pouted instead of looking chagrined, but at least he set the book aside and raked his eyes across all the monitors. "None of the alarms are going off."

Jane tapped the screen with the camera that had caught her attention. "About half a dozen people, all dressed in digis ran in through entrance 7 and used the employee service door. Didn't go to any of the shops."

"Digis?"

"Digitized camo, you dunce," Jane said. "Not all exactly the same. Surplus maybe?"

Lysle stuck his nose in front of another monitor that watched the employee access corridor in that section. The same group ran through, their backs to the camera and no weapons in sight.

"What do they think they're doing?" Lysle cocked his head watching. The group whipped around the far end, out of the camera's eye. "Sam should be closest. He can check them out."

"I didn't ask you for orders," Jane said. "If we start confronting every unfamiliar group who uses those corridors, we'll start bothering delivery men, who will complain to the vendors, and all the shops will pull their leases."

Lysle screwed up his face at her in disbelief. "That's a bit of a slippery slope. And if we do nothing and they end up causing trouble? You want to lose your job? I sure don't."

"Fine." Jane picked up the radio.

Sarah frowned when her daughter Julie snatched up the handheld radio in her pudgy toddler fingers. The radio crackled to life, making the girl squeal with delight. "Sam, this is Jane in control. We need you to check out corridor A15 near entrance 7. We see people on the monitor we don't recognize."

She pried the equipment from her daughter's grip. "Sweetie, don't play with Grampa's tools."

"It's all right," said Karl, Sarah's dad. "I can still hear it. Besides, that one's not mine. It stays here in the break room."

They sat eating sandwiches with one of the other security guards at the same kind of plastic table found in every breakroom. Julie had long since lost interest in her peanut butter and jelly and kept playing with everything else she could get her hands on. It made the others laugh, so Sarah allowed it. Up to a point.

"I don't want her thinking it's okay to play with work tools." Sarah set the radio on the table. "Besides, she's teething again. It'll end up in her mouth."

"Roger that, on my way," Sam's voice responded through the radio. Karl lowered his bologna on rye, and the other guard frowned.

Julie reached for the radio. Sarah deflected her hand with a circular arm sweep one of her jiu-jitsu instructors taught her. Who knew fighting techniques could be altered and used in parenting? She followed up the move by pushing the Gerber Graduate finger snacks closer. Julie let out some happy gurgles, grabbed the snacks, and stuffed one in her cheeks, making them poof out chipmunk-style.

Sam's voice crackled codes through the radio. The security guard groaned. Sarah asked, "Everything all right?"

"Just some weirdos exploring the employee access corridors behind the stores," Karl said.

"Not that." The guard took a bite and talked with food in his mouth. "Sam switched his radio to open mic again."

"Is that bad?" Sarah asked.

"No one else can use it as long as he's got it set there," the guard said. He swallowed, clearing up his speech. "You're the only one he listens to about this, Karl."

"I'm busy." Karl patted Julie on the head. She grabbed his hand and brought it to her face, planting kisses all over his palm.

"It'll only take a couple of minutes," the other guard said. "And Jane's just going to tell you to go anyway. And she'll put up more of a fuss, probably give you other assignments just for good measure. If you go now, it'll save time."

Karl sighed and set down his half-eaten sandwich. "Fine, I'll go set him straight. But you and Sam both owe me."

Sam reported as he passed the back of Claire's Boutique. He knew that shop well, as it was his daughter's favorite. He tapped the exposed bracers of the walls as he went by, his shoes surprisingly quiet on the concrete floor. He crossed over a stile that bridged some ducting and reported that he was near the intersection that should put the mystery group in sight.

There they were, huddled together at the locked door that led into the stockroom of Foot Locker, his son's favorite shop. He used the friendly approach. That always worked best, and it would allow the other security guards to hear through the open mic of his radio. "Hey there. You fellas lost?"

Smoke billowed from between them and they backed off. Sam rushed forward. "What are you doing!"

One of them pulled his hand out of a pocket, holding the same weapon Sam was supposed to carry but never did. He turned and ran back the way he'd come.

Good thing he'd switched his radio. He grabbed it off his belt and shouted, "They made a fire or set off a smoke bomb or something! They have a taser! Don't know what all else! Call the police!"

Zach ran after the pathetic security loser. When he was close enough, he stopped and lined up his shot, squeezing the trigger. The leads shot out. Score! The loser twitched, falling hard on steps over some sort of ducting. He closed in, expecting to have to hit him to keep him down. Instead, it looked like he'd hit his head on the weird bridge thingy. There was a cut on his face, and he was bleeding.

His friend fisted both hands on his head, like he was surrendering. His voice squeaked, "We're caught. This isn't working. You're never going to get your daughter back. And I'm fired!"

"Snap out of it." Zach gave him a shove. "We have cover. The smoke bomb will trigger the fire alarms. Everyone will panic and trample each other trying to get out. Follow the plan."

The others ran off to add to the chaos that was probably already spreading. Zach grabbed his friend's shirt. "Where's the breakroom they're in?"

His friend jerked away. "They're probably already on their way here!"

"Then show me a round-about way to get there."

"That was Zach's voice!" Sarah picked up the hand-held radio and shook it. "That was Zach's voice!"

"Easy now." The security guard popped a couple of Fritos in his mouth. "Calm down."

"Don't tell me to calm down!" She dropped the radio from her shaking hands and crossed her arms over the knot growing in her stomach. "He's coming for Julie! I just know it! He'll take her and I'll never see her again!"

"Joo Wee." Her daughter patted herself on the head. "Joo Wee. Joo Wee."

"I'm sure the police are on the way," the security guard said. "I'll go look for him."

Dad or Zach? She wanted to ask, but when she finally squeezed air through her closing throat, a plea came out. "Don't leave me."

"I'm sure your dad will be right back," he said.

Sarah grabbed her daughter. "I have to get her out of here."

"You don't know where your ex is," the security guard said. "You could run right into him. Just hide her in here while we handle this."

"Hide her where?" Sarah looked around the room. The table was open underneath, and a counter hugged one wall with full cupboards underneath. Some drawers. A sink. A fridge. The lockers for the security guards were all locked and inaccessible. She saw nothing she could hide her baby girl in.

"Just lock the door," he said. "Don't open it until your dad or I get back. Okay?"

Zach sprinted after his friend and had to grab him before he ran headlong around an intersection. "You have to check first. Always check first if someone is coming, stupid."

"This close, there's only one door," his friend said. "If someone's coming, it'll be either your ex with the baby, or her jerk dad."

"Or another security guard," Zach said. "A place this big with this many shops have to have more than just one."

A door closed with a loud click somewhere around the corner up ahead. Zach listened for footsteps. Instead, the fire alarm blared. He muttered, "Took long enough."

He peeked around the corner of the intersection. A security guard stood there, looking behind himself at the only door visible.

The man took a step back in that direction, calling, "Sarah! Change of plans. We have to evacuate."

That confirmed she was there. The guard had to go so Zach could get to his daughter. And he no longer needed a coward dogging his heels. He put a hand on his friend's shoulder and pushed him out into the intersection. The guard shouted, "Hey, you."

Zach aimed the taser at his friend, counting on the idiot not knowing it would have to recharge before it could be used again. He'd tell him later. They could laugh about it over beers.

The bluff worked. His friend got up and ran through the intersecting corridor. The idiot security guard followed, shouting after him to stop without even glancing in Zach's direction. He stepped out into the intersection. They were already gone. He laughed.

Zach stepped over to the door and tried the handle. Locked. He used his shoulder, and the door rattled. He pounded on it with a fist. "Sarah. I know you're in there. Open up."

Karl choked on smoke. He dropped to his knees beside Sam, both of them searching for the radio Sam had dropped. That had been Zach's voice coming through it, the little punk. *If only I'd taught him a lesson when I'd had the chance.* Was he in the building? Was he the one behind all this mess? If so, Sarah and Julie were in danger. Karl had to finish up with Sam and get back quickly.

Karl's hand brushed against the radio. He snatched it up and flicked the switch, turning off the open mic. He hit the push-to-talk button and said, "This is Karl, reporting in from the site of the incident. This channel is now free to use again."

"About time," Jane responded. "How big is the fire?"

"No fire," Karl told her. "Just smoke."

"Good," Jane said. "Everyone report in."

One by one, every security guard in the building reported in. Sam used his own radio to do so. Karl waited for a report from the breakroom. But the man he'd left there instead reported he had a perp in custody who turned out to be an employee of one of the shops in the mall.

Which meant Sarah was alone with Julie. With Zach somewhere in the building unaccounted for.

Jane's voice squawked once more. "That's everyone. Karl, Sam, you two get out in the promenade."

"Sam is injured," Karl reported using his own radio. "He needs the first aid kit in the breakroom."

"It's not that bad," Sam said into this radio. Blood leaked between his fingers where he pressed them against his forehead. "Just a cut on the head. Those bleed a lot. Looks worse than it is."

"Medical, police, and fire are on their way," Jane responded. "We've got chaos on our hands. The shoppers and clerks can see the smoke. Between that and the alarm, everyone is panicking and trampling each other. Get out there."

Sam coughed. "We gotta get out of this smoke."

Karl's cell phone rang with Sarah's ringtone. He pulled it out as he crawled after Sam to the nearest door out to the promenade. He hit the answer button. Before he could say anything, Sarah's sobbing hit him like a punch in the gut.

"Daddy," she cried. "Zach's at the door."

"Lock it," Karl yelled.

"I did. He's trying to get through anyway." Some muffled banging came through the phone. "I think he's ramming it or something. Come back. Help me!"

"You took self-defense," Karl reminded her. "Use it."

"I'm just a measly little white belt." Sarah's voice hitched, rising in pitch. "I've never even won a sparring match."

Sam went out to the promenade. Karl followed with Sarah screaming in his ear. Smoke billowed out behind them. It wafted up to join the tendrils already gathering near the vaulted ceiling twenty feet above.

People ran by. Some headed for an exit, but some went the other way, calling for someone. Children cried for their parents. A girl tripped and fell and was nearly trampled by the person behind her. And among them all, some idiots stood with their cell phones out, taking videos of the smoke.

"Who would do something like this?" Sam asked.

It was probably a rhetorical question. Karl answered anyway. "The guy who put my daughter in the hospital."

"I'll help here," Sam said. "You go get Sarah."

Zach backed up. He told himself the door was a linebacker on the opposite team trying to block him from the most precious football in the world. This time, when his shoulder hit, the door splintered from the frame around the latch.

Sarah stood in the middle of the room, pretty as ever, but with that look of superiority that always drove him crazy. He wanted to smack her for all the trouble she'd caused. Refusing to be riled like a child, he merely demanded what any reasonable father would. "Give me my daughter."

She threw a cell phone at his head. "Get out of here."

He ducked the phone and distracted her with talk while he looked around the room. "You have no right to keep her from me."

"The police think otherwise since you broke my ribs."

"It's not my fault you threw yourself at the table that way, trying to make me feel guilty." One of the cupboards under the counter along the far wall had a pile of junk in front of it, as if someone had swept out the contents in a hurry.

"I fell because you hit me!" She used that shrill tone that always made his skin crawl.

Zach shrugged. "He said, she said. The police only believed you because you're a woman."

The cupboard door bumped ajar from the inside. Was the baby in there? *Not even Sarah would have stuffed the baby in a cupboard! Would she?*

He shoved her aside and yanked the cupboard door open. There was his little girl. She held up her hands and squealed laughter. "JooWee hidey seek. Pway again!"

"Hidey seek a good idea." Zach reached for her. He would take her someplace she would be protected from Sarah for the rest of her life. No one would ever stuff her in a cupboard again.

Sarah kicked his leg. He turned to fend her off, to keep her from hurting the baby. She clawed at his face, but he pushed her away. She got up, so he backhanded her to keep her down. The baby's laughter turned to screams of terror. No child should have to watch their mother go berserk like that. Zach stood over Sarah, fighting the urge to kick her in the head. He pointed at Julie and shouted, "Now look what you've done."

Sarah shook on the floor. Her head spun from the smack. She had panicked. Reacted. Forgotten the last year of jiu-jitsu classes. She'd turned into the same gelatinous, cowering mess she always had the moment she'd looked Zach in the face. And now her daughter was screaming.

Sobbing, she pulled her feet under her. Was this the last time she'd ever hear her baby's voice? What was she supposed to do? He had beaten her countless times. She couldn't win a fight with him.

Zach grabbed Julie by the arm, yanking her out of the cupboard. Her screams shifted from fear to pain. All the videos Sarah had ever watched about shaken baby syndrome flashed through her mind.

No! Sarah would rather die.

She grabbed Zach's closest ankle and pulled. He reeled, off balance. Training kicked in, and Sarah pushed off with her feet, using his imbalance. He fell back under her weight, all the way, until his head whapped the tiled floor.

Her knee was on his belly before she even thought about it. She shifted to sit on him instead, high, so if he arched his hips he would have a harder time rolling her off. She crossed her arms to grab both sides of his shirt collar. Leaning in close, her head nearly touching the floor over his shoulder, she twisted her wrists. That squeezed his neck right on his carotids. Just like in class.

Unlike in class, her opponent never tapped her. His eyes fluttered up and closed.

Karl ran for the breakroom. There was a lot of scuffling noises coming through Sarah's cell phone. He could make them out even through Julie's screams. They had to be fighting, which meant Sarah was likely getting beaten again.

He burst into the breakroom, panting from his long sprint. Zach, the little punk, was lying on his back, knocked out by the looks of it. Sarah sat on his belly, leaning over his neck, pinning him and holding him.

She looked up. Zach didn't stir. Karl scooped Julie up in his arms, her cries softening but not quite stilling. Karl planted a foot firmly on Zach's chest and helped Sarah up. "That's my girl."

WESTERN

HIGH PLAINS MIGRATION

Written by Shelley Sperry
Edited by Larry Pass

The Wallace family arrived at the Exchange Bank in Ogallala in a dusty, unhappy silence when the morning sun was already burning bright and hot in a clear August sky. Sweat trickled down Mr. Wallace's long straight nose, but he didn't seem to notice. He held out a hand first to his daughter and then to his wife, helping them jump from the wagon onto the wood plank sidewalk in front of the bank.

Liza pleaded with her father, "Papa, can't you get Mama to change her mind? I don't want to go."

Sam Wallace shook his head as he wrapped the reins around a cedar post and patted the mare's warm neck. His stooped posture and the battered straw hat on his head told everyone he met that he was no rancher, no cattleman; he'd brought his family up from wheat country, at the southern border of the county.

"In near twenty years, girl, I've never been able to change your mother's mind once it's made up."

Miriam Wallace nodded and frowned at Liza. She was right about most things, and when it came to putting Liza on that train to the University, she'd never been surer of a decision. She sniffed and wiped her face and neck with a linen handkerchief, conscious she was in town now and ought to look presentable. Glancing up and down the wide dirt street and toward the white clapboard train depot, she allowed herself a moment of pleasure. She might just tell Mr. Wallace they should stay a little longer than planned and buy some pretty cotton fabric at the General Store too. Her younger daughter, who'd stayed back home with the chickens and new pups, needed a school dress.

"Let's go in. I don't know how long all this paperwork will take and we daren't miss the 10:35 to Lincoln."

Mr. Wallace coughed and spat a brown stream of tobacco into the dirt at his feet. "It's your pa's land you're taking the loan on," he said. "I can't see as it's anything you need me for. I'll be at Cowboy's Rest." Pushing his hat over his eyes and gesturing toward First Street, he spoke to Liza, "Come fetch me when you're finished."

Liza watched her father amble toward the saloon, a flush of anger in her cheeks.

On the front steps of the bank, Mrs. Wallace tapped her foot and gritted her teeth. Closing her eyes, she asked God to grant her patience and her daughter a less willful character.

Liza held tightly to her brown leather traveling case and bonnet, refusing to enter the bank.

"I'll wait here for Papa, thank you."

However, seeing her mother's temper rise as she twisted the handle of her small velvet handbag, Liza reluctantly followed Mrs. Wallace across the threshold.

The two women joined the bank manager at his desk in the front corner beneath a grand watercolor painting framed in gold called *Birds of the Great Plains*. A long-necked sandhill crane in flight filled the center with pretty songbirds and fierce birds of prey all around.

That is an admirable animal, thought Mrs. Wallace. *Sharp vision, endurance, and a taste for adventure in faraway lands. Not like one of those fat barn swallows.* Liza often said she liked the swallows for their colorful blue feathers and because they were content to nest and breed just about anywhere in field, forest, or town. They weren't particular. To Mrs. Wallace, they seemed very stupid indeed.

Gloves folded in her lap, Mrs. Wallace listened as Mr. Estermann, the bank manager, explained the fine points of the loan and made neat black x's exactly where she had to sign. As if she couldn't see the word "signature" with her own eyes.

"Now, are you sure your pa wouldn't have wanted you to keep this land debt-free, ma'am? He did a lot to keep that farm going after the '88 blizzard. I feel obliged to ask again..."

Mr. Estermann kept his lips firmly closed when he smiled and looked down at his customers from behind a polished mahogany desk. Liza shifted uncomfortably beside her mother.

"Yes, I am sure," said Mrs. Wallace. "My pa would be happy to send Liza to the university in Lincoln, just as he was happy to send me. And you know that's the truth, Jim Estermann, because you knew him well. The sooner she stops reading dime novels about those hellion gangs riding up and down from the Red River to Scottsbluff—all up to no good—the better. And now the newspapers have been telling us for the past month about how those Bullock and Campbell gangs are headed our way. It's better for Liza to read Mr. Emerson and Mr. Wordsworth and..."

Liza smirked. "That certainly did you a lot of good, Ma. Didn't it? Are you thinking about Mr. Thoreau when you're out hunting coyotes?" Her mother gave her an un-Christian look but did not reply.

Mrs. Wallace continued, "We cannot wait much longer, Jim. I need my money today before the 10:35 eastbound."

"You'll have it. But I'd be careful of taking the whole $50 on the train, Miriam. You don't know what could happen once you're outside the safety of these four brick walls."

"We'll take precautions. Thank you, Jim." She signed the papers on every line he'd marked, and snapped, "Now let's move on along so I can get my money."

Mr. Estermann grunted and assured her she'd have her money within a few minutes if she and Liza would like to take a seat.

Mrs. Wallace stood and motioned for Liza to follow her to the oak bench in front of the bank where they might try to catch a cool breeze. The street was quiet, what with the fall roundup still a few weeks away. They saw only two young ranch hands walk by, both on the way to the saloon where Mr. Wallace was still waiting.

"I've decided I would like to take a later train, Mama," said Liza in the honeyed, wheedling tone that usually persuaded her father but rarely her mother. "I truly appreciate you wanting to send me off to better myself, but surely it would be easier for you and Papa if I were home to help with chores and taking care of little Millie for another few weeks until the term starts." She smiled and patted her mother's bare, freckled hand.

Mrs. Wallace gripped both Liza's wrists tightly. "It's already decided, girl. You're getting on that train in—" She glanced at the clock at the top of the depot, "fifty minutes, give or take, and that's all there is to it." She took a breath and loosened her grip, searching her daughter's eyes. "I know you're afraid; I was too. But you must trust that I know best. Can you do that?"

Liza turned her head away, staring at the dust swirling around the train depot at the end of the street.

"I'll go get Papa. I'll tell him you just want to show him up, show everyone it's your land and not his, and that's the only reason you want the mortgage. He'll let me stay."

Mrs. Wallace's voice was a whisper as her grip tightened again. "If you try to speak to your pa, I will tell him what you and the hired man have been up to, and that will be the end of Robert. Won't it?"

Liza pulled her hands away as her voice reached a higher, more desperate timbre. "There's no sense in mortgaging that half section when I don't even care about going to college. I can teach at the school in Paxton without any fancy degree until I get married and still live with you and Papa. I want to start my life, not waste four years learning to name plants in Latin and recite poems about clouds. What good did that ever do anybody?"

Mrs. Wallace held her breath for a moment, gathering her thoughts and looking at the girl in front of her. She was so determined to build a nest on familiar ground, like those useless swallows she favored.

"You don't have to read books about botany or memorize poetry, but I will not let you throw your mind away before you've discovered what it can do. Nothing good can come of just staying where you are because it's easier or safer. You may decide to come back, but I won't have you back until you know what the fields and the sky look like beyond Keith County."

Liza sat still, her eyes closed. Mrs. Wallace felt her daughter's pulse race and finally slow again.

Mr. Estermann called Mrs. Wallace back to his desk, and Liza silently joined her. When all the paper rustling was done and the ink was dry, Mrs. Wallace offered a hand to Mr. Estermann to complete the deal.

Mrs. Wallace had just nestled the small envelope of money into her handbag, next to the precious Letter of Admission, when the sound of gunshots in the distance made her pause. She didn't want to believe it was more than some ranchers misbehaving as they rode into town, but she took time to say a quick prayer for the early arrival of the eastbound train.

To distract Liza, who had rushed to the door to see the commotion, her mother said, "Looks like it could get windy or maybe thunderstorm a little later, I wish you had an umbrella for your journey."

Liza sighed and said, "It'll be all right. I expect they have plenty of pretty umbrellas in Lincoln." Mrs. Wallace smiled to herself. Her daughter knew there was no sense in arguing anymore.

Liza put down her brown traveling bag next to her mother and walked out the door for a better view, exiting just as a rumble of laughter and another rowdy commotion started in the street. As she left, a bearded old cowboy pushed past her and into the bank.

"Howdy, Jimmy! Remember me?" The man was thin as a willow branch, with an eyepatch and a Bowie knife on his belt. He strolled up right beside Mrs. Wallace and slammed his hand on Mr. Estermann's desk.

Mr. Estermann stood, buttoning his jacket and fussing with his cuffs. "I... I'm so sorry, I can't say that I do remember. If you..."

"You don't remember? You don't remember foreclosing on my place last year and me watching my wife and boys take off for Kansas City? You don't remember that?"

The bank manager and all the customers within earshot held their breaths as the ruffian pulled the knife from its scabbard, laughed, and scraped a deep X across the polished desk. "Well, I remember you, Jimmy. I sure do. Real good to see you again."

Tipping his hat to all the ladies in the room, the fellow ambled out the front door. His laughter was replaced with the sound of thundering horses' hooves and gunshots firing in the street.

The front door flew open, and Mrs. Wallace watched a young ginger-haired outlaw, famous in all the High Plains papers as Red Campbell, waving a rifle like it was Independence Day. Behind him, she could see Liza standing on the sidewalk in front of the one-eyed cowboy who now had a sweaty arm around her neck and the Bowie knife at her throat. Her little girl was shivering like the last leaf on a cottonwood tree in December.

"All y'all git over on the other side of the room," said Red, ushering in two more members of his gang to herd the sheep. Mrs. Wallace recognized the bow-legged sidekick, Shorty Iverson, but the young one—who couldn't be more than sixteen—she'd never seen in the "Wanted" photos in the *Journal* or the *Sentinel*. One thing she knew for sure was that she hated them all. They had not bothered to shave in days, and they stuck their Colts in folks' faces in a way that was more than rude; it was prideful and arrogant. Worst of all, now they were standing in the way of getting Liza on that train.

Shuffling with the other customers toward the side of the room with no windows and no access to Spruce or First Street, Mrs. Wallace whispered to Mr. Estermann, "I expect you to stop this nonsense before someone gets hurt." He stared at her, and she shook her head. *He's a fool and a coward too. Why won't he do anything?* She felt a powerful urge to rush to Liza and draw blood from the man who held her.

"Hey, there! You look like you're in charge," said Red. And to Mrs. Wallace's surprise, Mr. Estermann gathered his wits and stepped forward.

"Yes. I am the manager here. We don't want trouble, Mr. Campbell, so please...you can put that weapon d-down. I can assure you that our vault can be unsealed only by the Wells Fargo team on Fridays. I am not able to open it, and we have no more than one hundred..."

"So, you know who I am? Good. You'd best stay quiet before you say something that puts you and everybody else here in an early grave. I ain't stupid, mister. I know about your vault, and I know you got a Union Pacific payroll in there ready to move tomorrow. You can open that safe with two combinations, and I got one of them off the Wells team in North Platte last night. You don't want to put up a fuss like they did. Do you? Just put in your numbers, and we'll be gone in no time."

Mrs. Wallace cleared her throat and interrupted before the manager could answer, "Mr. Campbell, I have no quarrel with you and neither does my girl out there. Tell your reptile to take his hands off her, so we can be on our way."

Red kept his rifle pointed at Estermann and motioned for the little boy of his crew to push the bystanders closer to the wall as he took a step toward Mrs. Wallace and grinned.

"You got quite a nerve, ma'am," he snorted. "Why don't you tell me what's in that pretty little handbag?"

Mrs. Wallace stepped back against the wall, suddenly aware that Red and his gang held Liza's life in their hands far more surely than she did. And yet she was still reluctant to let go. Not after all the years of working and planning for this day. She pulled the velvet handbag close to her chest for a moment until Jim Estermann gave her a small nod of encouragement. Maybe a gesture of submission might win some mercy for her daughter. She held the bag out to Campbell.

Red took the handbag and shoved her hard against the wall. Estermann rushed to help steady her while Red laughed as he looked inside and then tossed the bag onto the desk.

"Look there, boys! There's your gambling money for Saturday night! That girl will make a fine hostage for us to trade if the sheriff catches up with us before we lose 'em down in the Territories. Or maybe she'll make a good wife for Joe, the way he's holding on to her so tight! Ease up there, Joe!"

Two older women in the crowd at the back gasped and made out as if they were about to faint. Mrs. Wallace pushed Estermann away and stood up on her own. Feeling a roiling in her belly, she pleaded, "Will you do nothing to stop these devils, Jim?"

Red lowered his rifle for a moment, ordering Shorty to move Estermann toward the vault to start working the combinations. Then the notorious marksman raised the gun barrel again to rest it just under Mrs. Wallace's doughy chin.

"I ain't no devil, missus. I'm just a man doin' his job. So is your friend Jim, for that matter. You'd be smart to follow his lead so nobody has to die today. Now get over there next to him. You and your mouth gotta get locked up with all the rest of these fine citizens after we get our money."

Red and Shorty went about their business methodically, rounding up the half-dozen customers and herding them with Estermann and Mrs. Wallace near the back wall next to the vault door.

Shorty wedged his pearl-handled pistol between Miriam's shoulder blades as she began to argue again, and she finally stopped resisting.

After Shorty entered the first set of numbers, Estermann hesitated, and Red got impatient. "Joe's got the gunpowder to blow it open, but I don't think you want all these folks blown to pieces. Do you? It's your choice, mister."

Estermann shook his head and with trembling, sweaty hands entered the final combination, synchronizing the locks.

A bell hanging three stories high in the steeple of the Methodist Church clanged ten times as Red pulled the door open.

A brass spittoon flew from Mrs. Wallace's hand to strike Red squarely on the ear and knock him off balance. Cursing and wiping blood and tobacco juice from the side of his face, Red turned on Mrs. Wallace in a rage, wrapping his dirty fingers around her arm and pulling her to the far side of the room, away from the rest of the whimpering captives.

"Hey now, Red!" yelled Shorty. "Remember we ain't killing nobody that ain't armed no more. Right? You shoot her, and we'll have lawmen from here to Chicago after us. Let's just take the payroll and git out."

Mrs. Wallace's voice still quivered but her movements were slow and sure as she fell to her knees in front of Campbell. "You have a chance to do good and be granted mercy by God if you have mercy, too. Take the money, all of it, and leave the people be."

She turned her head to speak directly to the one-eyed hoodlum holding her daughter. "Take me instead of my daughter. She's a useless girl, but I can be your eyes and ears on the way to Santa Fe. You'll be a true Christian if you..."

She saw a light flash in her daughter's eyes, a light she'd rarely seen these past few years—a spark of love and gratitude.

Red looked hard at Mrs. Wallace and laughed. "Get up, woman, and stand against the wall. Maybe I should take you both—the girl as a hostage and you as a pack mule."

Shorty and the boy gathered as much of the payroll as they could carry in two linen bags, shoving a few pieces of jewelry and a fine gold watch into their vest pockets. Red told Joe to keep his revolver trained on the bank customers while he took charge of Liza, an iron grip on her right arm. She was shaking less, but tears flowed down her cheeks as she kept her eyes fixed on the floorboards. She stole an occasional glance at her mother until Red snapped her head up with a sharp pull on her auburn hair.

"Your ma don't want us to take you on our ride, but I bet you'd like to go. Wouldn't you? You read them dime novels, like all the girls. Don't you? You read about me and Shorty in the papers?"

Liza stared at him, a spark of defiance in her eyes now, and shook her head.

"Well, if you're nice enough, we might let you go when we get close to the border. Don't need you draggin' us down. You boys done in there? We been here too long, and the sheriff's bound to have a posse leaving North Platte by now. It's time to move!"

Joe herded the customers and bank manager into the vault, but as they tried to shut the door, Miriam pushed her shoulder into the breach. Her arm throbbed in pain, feeling as if it might break, but she ignored it, calling out for Liza.

"God damn you, woman! You want me to shoot that arm off?" Red raised his Winchester, but Liza thrust out with her left hand to ruin his aim. He spun around angrily, pushing her to her knees.

"M-Mama, it's okay. I'll go with him. Just do what they say and be safe." Liza's voice stuttered on the first syllable, but then she spoke true and clear.

Miriam shook her head and moved a step closer to Liza and her captor.

"I will not give up my girl's life when I've already spent seventeen years of my own to get her here."

"Holy Jesus, everybody git in the vault now and shut up. I've got a mind to kill you all."

But no one heard Red's words, muffled as they were by the rasp of steam and whistle of the Union Pacific announcing its arrival just as four deputies galloped onto Main Street. Miriam caught her breath, a sense of purpose now calming her own pounding heart.

The roar of the train was deafening for a few moments, and in the confusion, Miriam slammed the door of the vault shut with the half dozen other customers inside. She watched Shorty race toward the bank's open front door, only to be shot square between the eyes by one of the deputies outside.

The spittoon, still coated in Red's blood and brown tobacco juice, reverberated against a new target, and the one-eyed cowboy fell to the floor, gasping for breath. One vicious kick to his jaw from Miriam's sturdy black boot, and he was moaning on the floor, disoriented with his knife still in its fringed scabbard.

Liza pulled the next trick that laid Red Campbell himself on the floorboards. A knee to the soft spot between his legs set him squealing like a hog on the way to market.

Red recovered his breath and stood up, weapon in hand, ordering Miriam to stand beside her daughter. He kept his rifle trained on them, but directed his attention to the scene outside the front window.

The posse was now blocking the open doorway, revolvers and long guns cocked and ready. Behind them, the town had gathered, and Miriam could hear her husband shouting, "Let me through! Where are they?" and calling Liza's name.

"You deputies best hold your fire if you don't want dead women's blood on your hands," shouted Red.

Miriam rolled onto the floor, pulling Liza down with her and covering her daughter's body with her own. She yelled out, "Take your best shots against the devils, boys!"

The women held onto each other as a wave of bullets flew above them. Miriam felt as if she were trapped in a circle of hell with an unbearable noise and heat surrounding her. She could hear so many boots pounding and so many voices, including her husband's, shouting and crying out in the chaos. She raised her head to search for his face, but saw only shadows moving among the smoke.

When silence fell and she opened her eyes again, Red Campbell stood above her grinning, two new outlaws at his side with the boy sidekick lifeless at his feet.

Ambushed from behind, all four deputies and at least seven townspeople, including Sam Wallace, lay in pools of deep scarlet inside the bank. She could see Joe's Bowie knife glinting in her husband's hand, not four feet away from her and the one-eyed cowboy's throat slit nearly ear to ear.

Liza wept over her father in silence, and Miriam squeezed her hand tightly before Red pulled her away, breathing hard and unsteady on his feet. He pointed at Liza and spoke to the two gang members.

"Take this young one out to the horses, Lou. We still need insurance. Tex, you make sure we got our bags and whatever Shorty put in his pockets. Lock the old lady up with those folks inside the vault or shoot her. I don't care which. Then git to the horses as quick as you can. We'll ride hard. Should make it to the Territories in a week, so we can split up the take and make plans for Mexico."

Miriam felt her stomach rise up in her throat. She saw the glass over the clock on the wall had shattered and the hands were mocking her, paused at 10:22.

A pearl-handled revolver glittered brightly like a jewel a yard from her feet. Her eyes darted left and right, measuring the distance and wondering if she might buy a few more seconds to make a move.

"Mr. Campbell," she shouted, "I think Jim Estermann has a mighty big stash of money in his desk you forgot." Her voice was steady, but her hands were trembling.

Red turned, puzzled at the sound of a voice he didn't expect to hear again. He lowered his rifle for a moment, looking in the direction of the sound and then at the desk. Miriam lunged toward the revolver, screaming, "Down! Get down, Liza!"

Miriam closed one eye, gripped the Colt tightly, and felt the shot kick back against her. Red fired off his rifle, but he'd already been knocked to his knees by Miriam's first bullet. One of his shots hit the door and another shattered the front window. As her second bullet stopped Red's heart, Miriam saw the one he'd called Tex raise a shiny revolver and start firing.

The next ten seconds felt more like ten lifetimes. Hide, hide, hide, she thought. Pulling Liza with her and crouching behind the great mahogany desk, Miriam prayed she had at least two bullets left, or even three. She let Tex fire off one more. There was an ugly smell and a burning fire in her shoulder. Tex started walking slowly toward the desk, and as soon as she could peer over the top to see the knot on the red kerchief at his throat, she squeezed the trigger. He fell face down, blood flowing in a horseshoe around his head.

She rose up quickly, intending to save the last bullet for the one Red had called Lou, but she discovered nothing was left in the chamber of the pearl-handled revolver. But Lou didn't know that. When she looked up at the front door, the skinny coward was running toward a tall black mare and soon riding hard toward the west.

Liza stood up as a crowd of townspeople rushed in to view the carnage. Seeing her mother's handbag still on top of the desk, she opened it, pulled out the envelopes containing the money and the letter and slid them into her blouse before collapsing and kneeling beside her father.

Her mother stood nearby, listening to the train chug out of the station but certain that Liza would be eastbound before the week was done.

. . . . . .

In the letters Miriam scratched out each week in the kitchen, she told Liza about her sister's progress on the piano, the sermons delivered each Sunday, and Robert's misadventures with chickens and girls in Paxton. As far as she was able, she wrote charitably and with a kinder heart each year, even about the most foolish and un-Christian behavior of her neighbors.

Sometimes she dipped her pen in black ink and wished for green and violet and red, so she could capture all her feelings on the page. Sometimes she sketched the hawks and mule deer that ventured near the house, or the bare branches of the cottonwoods, listing each animal's and plant's name in Latin below. Liza said she liked seeing those pictures from home more than the photographs her sister sent.

Liza didn't come home that first Christmas and returned just briefly the next spring, now almost a grown woman. Miriam took that not as a reason for sadness, but as a sign she had won and that her daughter was a crane after all.

Miriam sat by her husband's grave at the First Methodist cemetery once a week to read Liza's letters from Lincoln. In due course, she read his daughter's letters about her graduate studies in Illinois and then from her new job in California. Miriam assured Sam that Liza would not remain a mere professor of Home Economics for long but would surely be Dean of Women in good time.

Ten years after her name became known from Salt Lake to St. Louis as the lady who helped vanquish the Campbell gang, Miriam Wallace boarded a westbound train with Millie, now eighteen years old herself. Miriam knew for certain she would miss the scent of cedars and the sight of rolling thunderheads in summer. But she quickly grew to love the sound of seagulls and preferred the taste of salt in the wind to dust and memories.

LOVE

I BRUSH MY TEETH LEFT-HANDED AND OTHER REASONS YOU SHOULD DATE ME

Written by Rebecca Monterusso
Edited by Danielle Kiowski

It was no coincidence I frequented that coffee shop on fifth and Jefferson. And how could it have been when their selection of tea was dismal, and they couldn't make a good latte to save the world?

But I went on a whim once and there he was, sitting at a table in the corner hunched over his laptop like the world around him had disappeared. He looked so cute in concentrated flow. It was as if light itself had done the physically impossible and bent in space just to be nearer to him.

I wanted to do the same.

Not that he was anything special. I've seen more attractive men, have even dated them. But you can imagine how unnerving it is to see someone who shifts your entire perspective of the world for seemingly no reason. You're almost compelled at that point to try and figure out why.

It's like your life starts to take on the quality of a movie and you let it play out through various scenarios trying to get it to reach an end you'd be happy with.

Sometimes you jump in, wanting to make it real. And other times, you let the fantasy take on a life of its own, knowing reality could never match up.

But damn if it wouldn't be nice to escape the reality of being single for once.

"You've got your whole life ahead of you." They say this as if there's a way to predict how long my life will last.

"You're so young. Give yourself time." Like I haven't already had my heart broken a number of times.

"You'll get it when you're older." As if the experiences I've already had don't count.

"It'll happen when you stop looking." Like I could ever stop looking and let fate take over such an important decision.

Most of the time I'd like to grab the proverbial "them" by the cheeks and scream, "Why the hell do I have to wait so long? Why should I have to get my heart broken so many times first?"

Nothing about it makes sense.

But there he sits. Every Monday and Wednesday. Week after week. Month after month as fall turns into winter. Same table. Same time. Never looking up from his computer.

If I could break the script—the one that says I should wait for him to approach me—I'd tell him it's not just coincidence that we both chose this exact spot to get some work done. I'd explain that I'm trying to give fate a nudge in the right direction, that an inkling of a forgotten memory tugs at me, begging me to tell him I brush my teeth left-handed.

And I'd ask him to picture this. We're in the tiny bathroom of our first apartment. It's late, after a long day of moving. We both want to brush our teeth and collapse onto the mattress sitting on the floor, wedged between towers of boxes labeled "our room." We're cranky, but we decide to get ready at the same time anyway knowing that the smallest of grievances could set us off at any moment.

Brush. Spit. Brush. Spit.

In hurried anger, silent but for the flow of water and plastic on teeth. Each expecting the crash of an elbow, knocking the other off-balance, an eruption of expletives fit for the mood.

But it doesn't come.

Our elbows never touch, and we finish cleaning off excess toothpaste. We turn to each other ginning, wondering why we'd been so ready to scream only moments before.

The transition into a new environment, one with less space and more concentrated emotions, is made easier by the simple fact that I brush my teeth using my non-dominant hand for some reason long forgotten, probably coincidental, but possibly related to the rules of time and space.

If that doesn't do it, I'd say I've been single my whole life, give or take a few dates. I have no crazy exes to contend with, no misplaced love or affection hanging around. You won't have to battle for my attention or wonder if I'm thinking of a different lover while in your arms. There won't be an awkward moment when we pass someone on the street who says hi to me but clearly doesn't want to impose, causing you to wonder if I've ever wished things had worked out differently, that the Universe had brought him to me instead of you.

I'd throw in the fact that I'm an avid reader. I don't need you to sweep me off my feet or be a knight in shining armor because I've loved a hundred fictional characters. And even though I've never felt it, I understand the difference between the messiness of real life, of choosing to love someone and being vulnerable, and fantasy, the wishful stories and hopeless romanticisms. I'd take the real over the imagined—most days.

Or I'd share the fact that children seem to love me. Since they're usually a good judge of character, you can be sure I'm not entirely crazy or secretly a serial killer. I think it's because I'm around their size which, side-note, means I'll never be taller than you, even in heels.

And, when we're in that tiny apartment learning to share our space—besides the sink, which I've already proven won't be an issue—all of these reasons ensure we'll have the tools necessary to make it through the things that break other couples.

I'd tell him that all he has to do is ask me out on a date. The rest is sure to work itself out.

So I go back. Each time I sit within his line of vision (more times than I care to admit to) trying to work up the courage to utter a single hello, to manufacture our own personal meet-cute, or to tell him all the reasons he should date me.

But I never do.

And one cold December day, after a week's vacation, I come back to find that he's stopped coming altogether. I drink watery lattes for three weeks staring at his empty seat, making small talk with an overly friendly barista before I opt to never return.

I often wonder if he'd still be going had I not disappeared, had I broken the unwritten script and bridged the silence without waiting for him to do so first.

Maybe the next time I see someone who sets my imagination off like a movie playing out in my mind, I can channel the version of myself most likely to convince me to say hello.

To tell the story of how I bent time and space to meet him and become the person I needed to be for things to work out between us. To let the possibility of love ruin the fantasy I've built up in my mind.

Probably something like this:

"A version of my future-self once reached through time and space to talk to my younger self. She told her a day would come when I met 'the one.' I'd know it by the fluttering stomach and rich imaginings of a tiny apartment. She convinced my younger self of all the things I'd need to do to prepare to spend my life with him, starting with learning to brush my teeth left-handed.

"She explained that, even though the skill seemed useless, eventually it would mean I'd never have to worry about sharing a tiny bathroom with a new love. And that had to matter in the grand scheme of things.

"And my younger self listened.

"Or, rather, events in her life—long forgotten by me as the rules of time and space prevent me from remembering time travel lest I blow the entire universe to shreds—gave me all the skills I'd need to live happily ever after like the stories I so cherish.

"Now, I've reached the point in my life where I'm ready to share those skills with someone else. I think you might be that person."

Maybe.

PERFORMANCE

JAWS

Written by Courtney Harrell
Edited by Melanie Naumann

The Pe'ahi cliffs lookout point was packed shoulder to shoulder by the time the sun crested over the eastern horizon, showering Maui's north shore with golden light. Big wave surfing fans eagerly waited for the day's spectacle on the legendary colossal waves. Tourists from all over the world slathered on sunscreen, donned oversized hats and bloated backpacks to slog down a muddy three-mile-round-trip, 4WD-only road in order to see what the hype was all about. Hawaii locals turned out in packs to support Maui's superstar and only female surfer to compete in a men's competition, fifteen-year-old Mele Kanaloa.

Most people around the world might not understand why this year's World Surf League Jaws Challenge was the most anticipated surf competition in recent history. But anyone who lived on the Hawaiian Islands or who had any kind of love for the sport of big wave surfing knew the extreme waves racing toward Maui at this very moment were created from what might be a once-in-a-life-time event.

Days ago, in between the Hawaiian Islands and the mainland, two Pacific winter storms had collided. Their powerful winds and rain forced unimaginable waves to speed across the ocean toward the Pe'ahi break. With a stroke of incredible luck, the NASA space station happened to be passing above the monstrous force of nature to witness the impact. The astronauts looming thousands of miles above Earth marveled at the imagery as if it were a CGI action movie. These reported conditions were every big wave surfer's dream and, at the same time, nightmare.

Wave size typically expected at the annual Jaws contest was around forty to fifty-footers, but today's situation, reported by the live wave observation center, was expected to peak at ninety to ninety-five-foot curls.

Kristina Kross, a.k.a. the Kraken, had purchased fading surf apparel company Rogue Riderz a few years back and aimed to grow her company and profits any way she could. That's how Rogue Riderz became the major sponsor of the Jaws Challenge. When news hit about the surge heading toward Maui, she insisted the organizers move the contest date to align with its arrival.

Once the competition was greenlit, all the surfers who had received invitations to compete purchased tickets and flew to Maui.

Spectators swapped stories of the waves they had ridden but none even came close to what they were about to witness today. Legendary big wave surfer Laird Hamilton smiled listening to many embellished claims but made no judgments.

All the safety responders had been vetted and prepared for this deadly competition. Ambulances with paramedics stood by a few miles down the Hana Highway connected by radio with a medical helicopter. Rescue boats, jet skis pulling sleds and even expert paddleboarders positioned themselves outside the lineup to watch, wait and be ready if any surfer needed them.

Most of the crowd admired the athletes who would perform today except for one sore loser, Shane Jackson. Shane had been a surfer for Rogue Riderz until a week before the competition when he broke his leg in an idiotic accident. Too much beer had been consumed and his bros threw too many moronic dares his way. All of which he accepted.

No one missed his absence from the competition because he was notorious for making crass comments on ESPN and in *Surfer* magazine that ridiculed his fellow competitors and sometimes teammates. Today was no exception.

Shane clutched a forty-ounce, muttered swear words and roared insults into a bullhorn, calling Mele an idiot for trying to compete with the "big dogs."

"Get that little girl out of there!" the bullhorn squealed feedback. "She can't handle Jaws."

He stood as firm as Haleakalā stood above Maui in his beliefs that Mele didn't belong, vocal about how no "female" could ever keep up—with these men or these waves. She'd get herself killed and spoil the competition for the real pros. While a few of his bro-fans fist-bumped him for "speaking the truth," the locals ignored the poser and held strong in their respect for Mele, their local hero.

Everyone on Maui knew Mele. She was extremely skilled for any age, but at fifteen she already exceeded 99.9 percent of the surfers in the world. Mele's parents had put her on the front of their boards before she could even crawl. By the age of three she could surf tiny waves. By age thirteen most waves were too tiny for her.

Her community of aunties and uncles remembered the moment she was born, held her close at age four when her parents died in a freak accident on the mainland, and joined in to help her Uncle Kai raise her.

Over the past few years, Mele's best friend, Jumpy, created documentaries of her wave riding and posted them on YouTube. Her followers revered her conviction that the ocean belonged to no one and riding waves was not about winning.

In Jumpy's latest YouTube doc, Mele had shared her plans to surf Pe'ahi on the predicted monumental day. But when the Jaws

Challenge shifted to the same date, only sponsored athletes in the contest would be allowed on the break.

The Kraken sought Mele out. Her pitch had been blunt. With Rogue Riderz sales struggling, the Kraken wanted to hook Mele's generation. She knew Mele wanted to be on those waves and could surf better than most any guy out there. Mele declined but the woman dangled an offer in front of her that was impossible to refuse. A $250k signing bonus and a guarantee to surf all the destinations Mele had drooled over her entire life.

All in exchange for joining the Rogue Riderz team.

The locals were puzzled to hear she had joined the lineup. Knowing her deep respect for the ocean, her drastic change of heart concerned her Maui ohana. Yet they wanted her to win.

The top surfers from around the world rested on their boards as the swell began to increase. They wouldn't have to wait much longer for the reason they were here today. The comforting shushing sound lulled their spiked adrenaline with its familiar calming vibes.

The guys were ready to compete. Most of them were impressed by Mele and gave her the shaka despite choosing to ride for the Kraken over the new and locally owned surf brand, Team Z, which had the smallest presence but was expected to take home a trophy due to their number one rider, Sion Sands.

On the other hand, her Rogue Riderz teammates ignored her. They were pissed their bro Shane was out and had been replaced by some girl. Long time mediocre Rogue Riderz surfer Bodhi Mills was not surprised the Kraken had gotten to her. Like her mythical namesake, what the Kraken wanted, the Kraken got, and she would take down anyone who got in her way. Mele was her latest prey. He knew first hand everyone could be bought, even Mele.

Joss Kross, one of the highest ranked competitors and MVP of the Rogue Riderz team who happened to be the Kraken's son, joked around with the other guys about Mele's lucky charm board and how crazy it was of her to show up. The rudeness of her own teammates threw Mele off, considering the respect surfers usually had for each other, so she kept her distance.

Sion waited on the boat outside the lineup with Mele. They had surfed alongside each other many days from sunrise to sunset. Fifteen years older, he had been one of Uncle Kai's first customers, a mentor to Mele at times, and now a friend. He could sense an anchor of heaviness weighing her down.

While Sion was here for the magnificent surf, he was also here to win. Having known Mele for so long, he knew she wasn't here to win, though she had the potential. He just didn't understand what had convinced her to join the competition. Whatever it was, he had a bad feeling.

Mele inspected her surfboard and best friend, Manō, named the day it was given to her. Uncle Kai wasn't just a surfer. He'd shaped his first board when he was twenty and started a business soon after. When Mele was six, he built her the nine-foot seven-inch board. Its size was cumbersome for a while but it became the only board she would ride. She felt that with the ocean around her and Manō by her side, she always had a protector and guide.

For as long as Mele could remember, all she dreamed of was surfing every big wave on the planet: Mavericks, Ghost Tree, Dungeons, Teahupo'o, Shipsterns, Tavarua, Cloud 9, Nazaré and more. But she couldn't burden Uncle Kai with the amount of money that would cost. He barely made enough selling his boards. But with the Kraken's offer, her dreams were in reach. All she had to do was agree to a one-year contract competing for Rogue Riderz.

That is, until this morning.

A sinking feeling clung to her. Sure, surfing the waves that felt larger than Mauna Kea made her want to vomit. But that wasn't the main reason her gut told her to screw the contest while her mind told her this was her opportunity to fulfill her destiny.

Her heart bobbed between the two, confused about which one was right.

A tsunami of dread drowned her after the Kraken changed their agreement. Just before she got in the boat to be taken out to the break, the Kraken cornered her. Mele was not to do her best. Joss had to beat her. If Mele couldn't abide by that agreement, all bets were off.

On one hand she thought it was insane to be paid and promised this kind of dream deal just to show up and not do her best. She didn't even know if she could win. But on the other hand, could Mele do this to herself, Uncle Kai and the community who had raised her? If she backed out now, she would lose everything including respect from everyone she knew.

If she didn't try her hardest could she die? It was one thing to disgrace herself, but these waves were not to be underestimated.

Mele stared at the horizon, ignoring everything.

Sion didn't interrupt Mele's thoughts at first. His blue eyes glistened from the rising sun. The boat rocked in unison as the wave swells grew a little bigger. Something made him wish he'd protected Mele. He didn't know what her agreement with the Kraken was, but he knew it must have been something big.

"I should have been there when the Kraken approached you. I hope Kai knows Team Z would have been honored for you to ride with us years ago. I didn't think that's what you wanted, so I never asked."

Mele didn't look at him. She couldn't believe he thought that's what was on her mind. She had never once thought about riding for Z or anyone. But now she had gotten herself into a mess she couldn't get out of.

"Give it your all today. Sure to make Kai proud, but more important for yourself. As much as I want to win today and see my name next to 'World record setter,' I know you have what it takes. And I would rather lose facing you than anyone here. You've been through a lot and this competition is yours to lose."

Mele looked at Sion. His sincerity was one of the things she liked most about him.

"I'll try," was all she could choke out.

Right on cue, the waves grew taller and the practice horn blew. Mele and Sion jumped into the water and paddled to join the lineup. One by one surfers began to seize waves, gliding down the face and warming up their bodies. The emcee revved up the crowd with an introduction of the day, the competition, and the stunning lineup. He ran through each surfer, a little bit of their history and their current season ranking. When he got to Mele's profile he couldn't contain his enthusiasm for the young newcomer and for her incredible bravery to compete with the men.

"And I'm just going to say what everyone who has seen this girl is thinking. Mele Kanaloa could take this whole contest. Already a legend at fifteen, she was born on these waves. Veteran Sion Sands, who is projected to win, told me this morning he believed in Mele."

The crowd erupted with cheers. Some people laughed, and others cried at the beauty of the ocean's natural gift. And so many voices came together for their hometown hero.

"Mele! Mele! Mele!"

Despite being a bit off shore, Mele could hear them. Her skin dimpled with chills from their belief in her. Her heart gasped a cry at their aloha. Her body ached to make them proud. That would have made this situation bearable and had been the original agreement.

A flush of heat numbed Mele's face knowing her performance today would be a lie.

She begged them to forgive her. She was not living the way they taught her. Mele squinted from the rising sun hoping to find Jumpy or some of her other friends but really needing the comfort of Uncle Kai's presence.

She had argued with him that morning. Not because he disapproved of her signing with Rogue Riderz but because he wanted to see the contract. Mele had defended the Kraken's insistence on handing it over after this first competition. Kai didn't trust that woman, and he was right.

Mele wanted to sink into the abyss.

Shane's irritating voice surged over her fans. "Look out behind you, Mele. You're gonna get eaten and spit out! You're just fish food!"

Sion nodded to encourage Mele to ignore him and grab some rides before everything started.

Half-hearted and already emotionally exhausted, she paddled up and over a few waves. Pretty soon the waves would be so large the surfers would need to be towed in to catch them.

Mele ran her hands over the smooth glossy top coat on Manō's surface and tugged on the foot straps she had added just for today. Manō wasn't the typical type of board the others used for big wave surfing, but he had spent more time in the water with her than anyone else. There wasn't a chance she would leave him behind on a day like today. But all the joyous rides they'd had over the years suddenly felt muddled by the reason she was out here.

She finally paddled toward the incoming wave, got on the backside, pushed off the lip, popped up and rode the curl to warm up her stiff limbs. For the next few hours, all she had to do was appear to do her best.

For a moment, she forgot about the competition and envisioned Manō cutting through the glassy Tahitian waves at Teahupo'o. The happiness of finding her way to this promised future was the only thing that could get her to focus. Finish today and she would have everything she ever wanted.

Two bursts of the airhorn ended the practice round. The announcer lifted a pair of binoculars and called attention to the infamous bomber sets of Jaws. "Oh wow, look at those gorgeous waves out there. Let's get this competition started!"

The first wave's hulking mass took the breath out of the spectators. Sudden fear for the safety of the surfers rippled through the crowd and some people hoped the competition would be called off. With nothing between the surfer and the fiercest of waves, one false move could be the end.

That morning, before the surfers were allowed in the water, the Kraken had not given a pep talk but instead a dictatorship of the order of performance for Mele and her three teammates. Bodhi was to catch a wave first and then Chase. She marked Mele third, leaving Joss in the cleanup spot.

The first heat was underway and the lineup erupted out of the gate so fast that Bodhi from Rogue Riderz and Lane from Ripcurl grabbed jet ski tow-ins at the same time elbowing each other for the wave. To nobody's surprise, Bodhi won the battle.

Mele was relieved to sit on the left, outside the narrow break, and wait her turn. Waves were ridden and almost immediately their scores popped up on a large digital board visible from the lineup. The guys so far had done decently. Sion was in first and Tyler from Team Lost was in second. Mele believed she could score pretty high. Yet she had agreed to do worse.

Every single second stretched into minutes as she waited for that "just right wave" to make her lamest efforts on.

Joss splashed up beside her.

"What are you doing? It's your turn. Go! I can't do anything until you've gone. Fuckin' grom." His insults made her fade.

Moving her arms through the water, she tried to psyche herself up but instead felt like she was paddling a sinking ship. Manō was angry and wanted to ride hard, but she had to deny that desire. She snuck a look to the cliffs where the Kraken towered in her perch, illuminated in her hot pink shirt, gripping her telescopic binoculars and Mele's future.

The Kraken peered at Mele and smirked. She was counting on the reluctance on Mele's face. Joss would win and become an international household star by beating the desired champion whose name had caught fire on the mainland.

Mele raised her hand to flag her tow-in.

She tossed Mele the line and encouraged her. "You're our girl. Ready?"

Mele couldn't even fake a smile. She just nodded and slipped her feet into Manō's straps. When the jet ski took off, Mele stood up and rode across the water like a wakeboarder. Her legs quivered like Jell-o. She carved back and forth getting used to her footing. Her driver nodded to let go of the tow line. For a split second Mele contemplated bailing out completely.

But she didn't. She followed the rules and kept it simple, riding the wave and pulling back, finishing with a moderate score.

Joss laughed at her performance, snatched the next wave and, after everyone surfed a few runs, earned a high-ranking score to end the first heat in third place.

When the horn blared to start the second heat, Sion waved to be towed in first. Once he dropped the rope, he zipped up and over the lip just in time to hop on the monster wave. He carved through the warm turquoise water leaving a white trail behind his every move.

The waves on a normal day at Jaws moved around twenty miles per hour, but Sion had a feeling today he was sailing twice the speed. He ripped through the wave gently cutting back and forth until his short but sweet ride neared an end. He had a near perfect score and enjoyed a healthy taste of competition, knowing he was the one to catch.

Joss' teammates insisted on being towed in next, sticking to the dictated order. They didn't do as well as Sion but good enough to earn decent scores from the judges. Mele wondered what these surfers were really capable of if they let their full skills shine. What would she look like?

A memory floated into Mele's head at how hard she had worked ten years ago to learn one of her favorite moves—a roundhouse cutback. She tried and failed over and over again that day. Uncle Kai gave her pointer after pointer until she fine-tuned the intermediate move into a gorgeous display of wave riding. She was so tired that night she slept fifteen hours before launching out of bed and back into the water to play with her new skill.

Mele's body began to sparkle with excitement and Manō was ready to do the work for her, amped up to ride the incoming wave.

Her body moved faster than her mind, realizing she had grabbed a tow-in to jump up and over the ginormous wave, which had to have measured at least seventy feet high, though the local scale would call it thirty-five feet. Wave measurements in Hawai'i were called out about half the size they would be anywhere else in the world. Some said it's because locals liked to under-value the wave sizes so when tourists get out there, they leave from intimidation. Others say it's how the locals keep the haoles away from killer breaks by saying they're too small, not worth riding.

Big wave surfing pioneer, Buzzy Trent, once said, "Waves are not measured in feet and inches. They are measured in increments of fear."

This made the most sense to Mele because today her fear was bigger than any wave she had ridden. But when she heard the chant of her name over the roar of the wave, she dove in, feeling Manō's excitement to race down the face and show off her masterful roundhouse cutback.

She was loving this moment until a hot pink flicker from the crowd stabbed her with the facts. She was not to outperform Joss. Period.

Mele's footing fumbled. She almost wiped out but somehow caught herself and recovered. The Kraken couldn't fault her for not dying out there.

Points would be docked for her mistake but at least it would be real.

Joss and his crew laughed at her. "That was some kind of riding out there. Lame riding for a lame ass girl. You're really bringing down the Rogue Riderz name."

Mele rolled her eyes and paddled away.

The judges' scores posted on the jumbo board and they actually weren't terrible.

With twenty minutes left in the second heat, Mele knew she had to catch at least two more waves to qualify her best of three attempts. The other guys were performing pretty well today, especially the OG surfer for O'Neill named Rush, but everyone seemed to be slowing down waiting for the waves to hit their peak.

A really nice wave started to come in and Bohdi jumped on the chance. He waved and was towed in. He barely crested the top before he lost his footing, crashed and disappeared.

One distinctive "oh!" filled the cliffs like a marine layer. His flotation vest popped him up in the whitewash right away. The jet ski emergency team rushed in to retrieve him just before another giant wave could take him under. He was safe but his face was stark white. They dragged him and his board to the sidelines.

Bodhi crawled into a rescue boat and was met by an EMT. He shook his head and shortly after was driven away.

Mele knew what that meant. Everyone knew. He had quit.

As much as she wanted to throw it back in Joss's face that she could hang while his bro couldn't, she would never want anyone to be injured or worse.

She looked out to sea where the sun hit a rainy patch in the most perfect way that the sky drizzled a vibrant rainbow.

The most beautiful wave emerged in the distance. It must have been at least an eighty-footer.

Shane's bullhorn squealed from offshore. "That's yours, Joss. Show that girl what big wave riding is really about."

Despite the fact that Chase was supposed to take the next wave, Joss raised his fist in the air. "Yeah, bro!" He turned in her direction and just couldn't stop himself. "You know, my mom only put you on the team to sell more clothes to little girls like you. Just admit you're not cut out for these waves and go home."

Mele gritted her teeth. Being a girl and being the youngest to ever ride these waves intimidated them. Why else would the Kraken want her to purposely lose? Because they all knew she had a strong chance of beating them.

The announcer's voice boomed that there were only three minutes left in the second heat.

Joss grabbed the tow line as the jet ski took off in the direction of the wave. But he made one last gesture by pulling the rope in such a way that he skirted toward Mele and sprayed a line of water in her face.

Right away, Mele waved her jet ski over.

"Take me in!"

"You can't. He grabbed it first."

The rules were clear. One rider on a wave at a time. For the judges' clarity, but even more for safety.

"He hasn't caught it yet!"

The rules also stated whoever peaked over the top first owned the wave. Her jet ski assist wanted to help Mele, so she took off full speed ahead and caught up to Joss' ride.

Joss growled. "This is my wave!"

But Mele was done taking his insults.

"Not yet!"

Mele and Joss met at the top of the wave—face to face, side by side, neither of them willing to budge.

She couldn't hear the cheers, the chants, or the judges reacting to the situation. All she could hear was the rush of the wave about to push her ahead.

Joss fought to maintain his line, racing parallel to Mele while trying to crest the wave first. She had faced groms, posers, and pros her whole life, and she'd learned early on how to claim a wave. She wasn't about to let him snatch this ride.

She careened ahead and pulled off an ill-advised roundhouse cutback at the top of the wave directly in his path. She saw the look of fear in his eyes right before Manō's nose pearled under water.

For a split second Mele had no regrets.

Until they both lost control. Bodies over boards, leashes twisting in a tangled mess, they toppled down the backside of the wave.

She didn't have time to activate her flotation vest before the next wave rushed over them. Leagues of water deep-sixed them toward the underworld.

Sion was the closest person to the accident and he didn't hesitate. Ripping off his leash and tossing his board aside, he raced out to where he saw them land and dove down.

She went downward as Manō went upward, the leash pulled to choose between the two.

Three minutes. That's the amount of time a typical person could live without oxygen.

Emergency jet skis zoomed round and round looking for Mele and Joss. In no time, several more waves had pounded over where they landed and the chances of them being found alive were dimming.

A floating calm washed over Mele, ready to wrap her in the ancestors' arms. But she snapped back, her heart pounding to remind her how well-practiced she was at holding her breath for long periods of time. Because moments like this happened.

The announcer's voice boomed through the speakers that the competition was on pause and for everyone to please stay calm while the safety team did their job.

Moments later Joss's board launched out of the water directly upright before falling on its side. Joss popped up next to it gasping for air.

Beneath the waves, Mele reminded herself to relax as her hands found the four tabs on her safety vest and pulled them one by one. Her body rocketed to the surface popping her up in the whitewash near the far-right corner of the break.

Emergency responders zoomed over and lifted her onto the jet ski sled.

As they sped out of the crashing wave, a name spread through the crowd.

Sion.

Mele looked in every direction.

"Where's Sion?" she asked the jet ski driver. The driver nodded in the direction of the rescue boats where Sion was being lifted in.

The announcer commented on the play-by-play actions occurring in the water, peering through binoculars to see Sion's bleeding leg.

The horrified crowd went silent, assuming the worst had happened. Almost every person in the world had one thought when they entered the open ocean. And this location had its name.

Jaws.

The commotion from the crowd grew. Fans by the hundreds were crying out.

Shane didn't care that something graver had happened. His obnoxious bullhorn screamed. "Yeah, my boy's okay!"

Mele followed Sion to the medical boat while Joss got on another one so all three could be checked out. Mele removed her leash and strapped Manō to the side of the boat. An EMT scanned her but she pushed him away.

"I'm fine. Help Sion."

Sion's calf gushed blood.

Another EMT cleaned the wound. Sion began to laugh at the look on Mele's face.

"It wasn't a shark. I got sliced from one of the fins on Joss' board."

"Are you sure?"

"I was there. Wasn't I?"

"Yep. One clean slice," said the EMT. "You need stitches. That's something I can't do on the water." The EMT hopped on his walkie and called to the stand-by ambulance that they had a surfer who needed to go directly to the ER.

"So what are you saying?" cried Mele. "He's gotta get back out there. He has to compete." She grabbed Sion's hand in hers. "You're the best and you're going to win."

Sion shook his head. "I think today isn't my day."

Tears slid down Mele's tanned cheeks.

She thought about all the poor decisions she'd made recently and how, if she hadn't gone against her beliefs, she wouldn't be in this mess and Sion wouldn't be injured. This was all her fault.

"Hey," he said. "That was a radical move you pulled. You have to take risks in life. And sometimes things go wrong. But you have to get back out there and do it again."

"But if I hadn't challenged Joss for the wave, you'd still be in the competition."

"I chose to swim out and I'd do it again. Never stop taking risks when they feel right in your heart." Sion smiled.

The EMT walked between Sion and Mele to put an ice compression on his bandaged calf.

Sion said one more thing. "Whatever got you out here to compete, don't let it send you down a path you never meant to go."

Another boat pulled up beside them and a voice perked Mele's ears. The Kraken.

Joss whined but his mother refused to listen. She had seen everything and wasn't pleased with the newcomer's inability to follow directions.

With a wave of her hand, she commanded Mele to her boat.

Mele hugged Sion and crawled over the rails, dragging Manō with her before his boat sped away.

The Kraken sent Joss back into the water before she spoke.

"You haven't forgotten our agreement. Have you?"

Mele shook her head.

"What would everyone think if they knew their girl sold out? I could tell the news stations how you approached me with a list of demands in exchange for a contract because you couldn't wait to get off this island wasteland. Your fans would drop you instantly. Your reputation would be ruined throughout all of Hawaii. And most of all you would break Maui's heart. You'd always be a fraud and your Uncle Kai's business would be ruined."

"That's not what happened!"

"Shall we test it out?"

Her threats wrapped around Mele's throat like tentacles.

When all medical personnel gave the go-ahead to continue the competition, the announcer started the third and final heat. The final ranking and winner would be determined by the outcome of these last twenty minutes.

Mele paddled to the lineup, still shaken from the Kraken's warning. Guys riding for various teams came to check on her, but no one knew what was really troubling her. Even Chase from her own Rogue Riderz team spoke to her, but not Joss.

The air horn blared and the third heat commenced.

One by one, the surfers took off. Even though Mele and Joss had skirted breaking the rules, neither were docked points. The judges discussed it a bit and since neither of them had officially "gotten" the wave and no one was injured too badly, neither were DQed.

The first few guys rode the waves beautifully and scored personal bests.

Mele punched the water and yanked Manō's leash. Ride the waves but don't do her best. If this was just the beginning, what would the Kraken demand when she was on the competition circuit?

She patted Manō and waved to her tow-in, no longer caring about some stupid "order."

"I'm glad you're okay," she said to Mele.

Mele shook her head and apologized. "I'm sorry. I let Joss get under my skin. I shouldn't have pushed you to take me in. I hope you didn't get in trouble."

"Not at all. You were right about the rules. You both had the right to go for it. Just don't let Joss or anyone provoke you. These are serious waves. Just focus on you."

Mele nodded and readied herself as they took off. The water under her board felt different or maybe it was Manō. She could sense her best friend wasn't happy with her retaliation. But she was already on her way to catch a seventy-five-foot wave.

Manō lifted her up and over the wave. She dropped the rope and together they plunged down the face in a direct line, slicing through the water. Cutting back and forth, Manō's fins guided every move. They chased the endless wave, living for every single breath of salty air and speed.

Mele exhaled to let go of the things the Kraken said. She had no control over this woman.

A loud crack ripped through the air, but Mele didn't stop. Back and forth, they created a wide zigzagging path until she reached the end.

The crowd cheered voraciously for Mele and Manō, who she felt was the real athlete. She rested on her board to wait for her lift, but the feeling that something was off with Manō returned. Her feet dangled on both sides of the board and when she looked at her companion's body, she saw what was wrong.

A small crack had ripped through the width of the board. It looked minor, yet the longer she sat there the more prominent it became.

A jet ski revved toward her to give her a ride but she felt the lower half of her board sink while Manō's upper half stayed flat on the surface. The fact that she had completed the ride made no sense.

Her tow-in pulled up. "Grab on!"

Ocean spray showering her face told her they needed to move fast. She grabbed the jet ski side handle and, before she had a tight grasp on Manō, they took off.

Her board flopped behind them the whole way to the boats on the other side of the break. Looking away for one second, the leash around her left ankle felt lighter. When her eyes returned to her board, only half of Manō's body dragged behind.

"Manō! My board!"

The jet ski slowed down.

Tears filled Mele's eyes as she pulled her leash in and hugged Manō's half body. The other half sloshed in the water by the lineup of surfers, left alone to bleed out its fractured core.

She couldn't believe it. Manō had given up on her.

A gasp from the crowd stabbed Mele even harder.

The announcer commented how this just didn't seem like Mele's day.

But the competition didn't stop for her this time. Her teammates and the other guys continued a fierce fight to raise their score during the last ten minutes.

Uncle Kai's boat bobbed up next to Mele. With one half of her companion tucked beneath her arm, Mele crawled into the boat. A few moments later, a rescue paddleboarder delivered the other half.

Uncle Kai didn't give her a lesson or tell her to get back in there. He just wrapped his arms around her shoulders and held her close.

Her tears fell heavily. They had nothing to do with the competition and weren't only about Manō.

She had kept a terrible secret—one that affected not just her but Uncle Kai, too.

But he knew her better than anyone in the world.

"When your parents died, I was shocked they had named me your guardian. I was just a surfer. I could have named a hundred better people to raise you, but they knew the only thing you needed in life was exactly what I could offer. You knew what you wanted from the day you were born and you've never wavered. Riding, not competing, is what you are meant to do."

Mele knew he was right. Literally nothing else in the world made her feel complete. Surfing wasn't a sport to her. It was like breathing.

"Manō's gone," she whimpered. Manō was the only reason she could surf the way she did. Now that was all over.

"So? I shaped Manō for you when you were six. You rode thousands of waves before then. Manō's a board and he knows you no longer need him. There are a million boards in the world. You think Laird Hamilton rides only one board?"

Mele shook her head.

"He's here, you know. Laird."

Mele's eyes went wide. Her all-time hero and the true local star was in the crowd? Laird was the best of the best. He had surfed all the waves around the world she wanted to ride and had ridden on that historical day at Jaws when the waves hit one hundred feet.

"I...I didn't bring a backup board."

Uncle Kai shook his head. "You think I come unprepared?"

He uncovered a board that wasn't anything special. Just a board he made a while back that Mele had tested out for him. It didn't have a name or any remarkable memories. It didn't give her the zing Manō did.

She hung her head low. "I can't."

"You know, every choice that comes to you presents two options. Once you make a decision, you head down that path. Sometimes you go a way you wish you hadn't and the further you get away from your true self, the more likely you'll feel lost. But even when you feel lost, you're presented with two options. One of them can get you back on track."

Mele squinted at Uncle.

"If the reason you chose to be out here today was to win a contest, you're unlikely to win at this point, but so what! There will be plenty more. But if you came here to ride the waves, there's one more just waiting for you. Maui will love you no matter what you choose."

While the other riders continued to fight for the win rather than the waves, Mele knew she had veered off her path.

But Uncle Kai was right. Mele had two options in front of her. Keep the Kraken's offer or get back out there for herself.

She gently removed Manō's leash from her left ankle and ran her fingers over the thick ban of lighter skin that suddenly felt naked.

Screw the Kraken. That deal was done. If the Kraken tried to ruin Mele's name, she'd bring herself and her company down too.

Mele chose herself because she wanted to create a new path for the life she wanted.

She ripped off the Rogue Riderz-logoed rash guard she and her former teammates wore and threw it on the boat deck.

Uncle Kai smiled and handed her the new board.

"This one rides just like Manō but the power isn't in the board. It's in you."

Mele attached the new leash to her ankle, hopped in the water and paddled to the lineup.

The double air horn blew, signaling the last three minutes before the competition ended.

The announcer's surprise was evident when he noticed Mele in the water. "Wow, folks! Not only is local Mele Kanaloa back in the water after a string of difficult upsets, but it appears she is no longer wearing a Rogue Riderz jersey."

Her local supporters cheered. Jumpy and Mele's posse bounced up and down.

Mele threw a shaka in the air to let Maui know she loved them.

Joss smirked and flipped her off. Mele chose to smile, watch, and wait.

Lane busted out a big ride on the next set followed by Lost's Tyler. The other surfers in the competition gave it their all and some of them rode well. Others did decently while some wiped out.

Still, Mele waited.

The air horn blared one long sound that echoed across the Pacific Ocean and up to those NASA astronauts. The whole world knew the Jaws surf competition was over.

And that's exactly what Mele wanted.

Everyone was exhausted. Not just the surfers in the water but the judges, the announcer and everyone who had come out to support.

The surfers paddled to the boats receiving cheers and admiration for their incredible efforts.

The lineup emptied of everyone except Mele.

Uncle Kai knew what she was up to.

The crowd started to disperse until Jumpy called out Mele's name. Everyone turned to watch.

In the distance, a rumble grew. The mythical swells offered one last gift as the most epic wave emerged. She knew this one hit the peak of the day—a gorgeous glassy wave measuring ninety-five feet.

It was bigger than she or anyone out there had ridden, except for Laird.

Her tow-in zoomed up to her.

"Are you about to do what I think you are?"

Mele's eyes zeroed in on the wave. Manō wasn't with her and never would be again. So it was time to find out if what Uncle said was true. Her skill didn't come from her board but from within.

Mele grabbed the tow line, stood up and wiggled her body to feel the water beneath this new board. It felt different but this was one of those many moments she recognized where she had two paths. She had chosen the new path by backing out of her agreement, which meant she lost the other perks. But she knew none of that mattered. When she one day surfed those majestic waves around the world, it would be on her own terms.

Mele steadied herself as the jet ski drove to the back side of the wave. She zipped to the top, anchored into the board and released the rope.

And she jetted down that wave like no one had. Cutting through the slope of clear turquoise water, she felt truly like herself. This moment filled her with the ultimate rush of what life was about. Mele knew wherever they were, her parents were proud of her.

The wave curled over in the most spectacular barrel to hug her. The noise from her fans was muffled by the tube. This ride was just for her. She pumped her left foot to encourage the nameless board to race even faster.

The barrel closed in quickly but she had no fear. She and the ocean were one.

The crowd sucked in a unified breath, afraid for Mele as the wave neared the break.

But one big cheer shook the cliffside as Mele punched through the gigantic face, sprinted ahead of the collapsed water, beat the white wash and pulled off to the side to meet her ride.

She let out a howl that echoed all the way to Hana and back.

The sea of fans bounced up and down and Jumpy had captured every second. He turned in Shane's direction and yelled, "That's my bud!"

The judges and announcer were speechless.

Once she reached Uncle Kai's boat, she was illuminated with love and the reminder of who she was.

"Mele! Mele! Mele!"

Uncle Kai beamed at her.

The Kraken clenched her teeth and pounded the letters on her phone to shoot a text to Mele that said "Deal's off!" But Mele wouldn't look at her phone anytime soon. She knew what awaited her and couldn't care less.

The judges handed over their final scores and the announcer read them off.

Mele didn't win. She had been disqualified ultimately for quitting her team. And that was just fine with her.

Actually Joss didn't win either. Sion would have taken the top prize if he had finished the contest, but instead Rush took first for O'Neill. Lane took second for Ripcurl and out of everyone, Chase from Rogue Riderz took third. Joss didn't even place.

Chase would be fired before the day's end but was over the lying and scheming, anyway.

Mele knew she would never forget Manō, but amidst the loss she'd gained something that could never be taken away from her.

SOCIETY

ABOVE ALL ELSE

Written by Shawn Coyne
Edited by Tim Grahl

What was once subjectively qualitative had now turned formulaically algorithmic.

The days of incubating timeless, idiosyncratic stories for passionate and demanding niche readerships turned into "net sales probability analysis." And as one book publishing season bled into the next, *The People's Press'* founding ambition to become a meaningful human story incubator bled with it.

Now the *People's* publications had underlying data analysis as keenly wrought as a highly leveraged quant fund. Whether target marketing the next paranoid thriller to urban singles on holiday break, a forbidden guilty pleasure love story to rural telecommuting lonely hearts in the Midwest, or even the most celebrated *Iowa Writers' Workshop* graduate's Nabokovian postmodern anti-novel to nihilistically inclined Millennials still living at home, the *People's* output proved remarkably financially predictable.

The return on the *People's* investment held steady.

The price paid for such consistency? Releasing the kind of works that built the company's infrastructure and allowed it to weather underperforming periods in its early lean years—titles written, edited and designed for a particular group of readers desperate for innovations of their favorite genres—was now anathema.

Small beer.

Ten quarters prior, the *People's* "tie-breaker," Pat Algernon, decreed that the company's wimpy goals to achieve reasonable profitability across multiple genres was irrational. It had bred, as she'd so eloquently titled her report to the shareholders, *A Culture of Mediocrity.*

But the opening salvo from that document's accompanying speech cemented her reputation as book publishing's realistic quantitative strike force.

"How were *The People*," she began, "to survive in the era's shockingly disruptive book publishing environment? How would they come to terms with an eroding marketplace? If they didn't shoot for the top of the commercially viable pyramid, they'd cease to have the opportunity to pursue their editorial bliss. Simply put, books need to make money. No money. No books. The game has changed, and *The People's Press* has to change with it."

Now just two and a half years into her five-year plan, the *Press* strived to publish the books that would appeal to everyone, those with the "quantifiable potential to appeal to the broadest possible audience." This drive for the multi-million-copy bestseller assumed prominence because, as Algernon so convincingly explained, mass popularity added shareholder value today. Long-term value delivered light years away in some distant fantasy world where evergreen "masterworks" sold year after year as a business model was ridiculous.

So under Algernon's directive, *The People's* editors intently fixated on cultivating what the industry referred to as "the agent community" to find the next big thing. And the number of expense-able breakfasts, lunches and drink dates with WME, ICM, and the like became the currency of an editor's go-get-er-ness in the company.

Fewer and fewer of this new breed of editor remembered the days when Tom "Old Paint" Dachson developed the company's first published masterwork. Back when the publishing house came online as an alternative throwback, he and his crew of mentees scoured the Internet to find the nexus voice of an up-and-coming sub-sub-sub-genre popular amongst a hardcore group of readers. Three years and eighteen drafts later, all soberly and meticulously edited using Dachson's distinctive methodology, the writer Melissa Ford delivered the result. *Fulcrum's Apotheosis* was an alternative universe action labyrinth story of a young female Christ figure that satisfied a hungry audience.

Financially, it did marginally well its first year, just a stitch over breakeven. No great shakes, but respectable.

But then, something unexpected happened. *Fulcrum's Apotheosis* doubled its first year of sales in its second year. And with nineteen years of added compound growth to follow, *Fulcrum's Apotheosis* stood alongside *The Da Vinciana Code* as one of the bestselling novels of the previous century.

Alas, *Fulcrum's* creator now lived in the Hollywood Hills and hired protégés to "writer-room" her novels from idea to finished manuscript. She'd long since left *The People's Press* for, as she put it, "a more traditionally aggressive publisher." The Rolls Royce of publishing, Infinitum House.

Dachson took Ford's departure hard, got a bit bitter, resentful even. But he was nothing if not a survivor.

Yet, "Old Paint" remained with the *People* through thick and thin. His sobriquet, the compliant horse breed known for its desire to please its owner, was coined by founding revolutionary partner Maria Harris Jones. But that was before her "comeuppance" at what the older employees referred to in hushed tones as the 2020 Tuesday night editorial massacre. After the debacle,

Dachson pledged to himself to disengage from publishing's politics and to "work harder."

While a shadow of his former editorial self, he still had the acquisition touch, figuring out what would sell and acquiring it cheaply from his old crony agent relationships and naive writers. But the days of him doing nine-hour conference calls walking a writer beat by beat through his edits were long gone. Putting that much into a single project was rather pointless in this day and age.

Over time, it became an unspoken understanding that "Old Paint" was best left alone until 10:30 a.m. One had to allow for the time it took for his hangover cure—three Leberkase and Limburger cheese sliders he had an assistant editor pick up at the Weimar food truck in Alphabet city washed down by a pot of black French press coffee—to do its magic. Also, one learned not to take him too seriously just after his return from an agent "lunch" when he was quite animated and entertaining. He tended to forget what exactly anyone had said to him, especially what he had said to them.

Even though he graciously expensed all of the drinks, one just never went out with him for afternoon cocktails. If discovered too often in his company, one risked a label of Old Paint's rummy-in-training.

That said, between 10:30 a.m. and 12:30 p.m., Dachson was intellectually superlative, the most exceptional editorial mind in the business. Bar none.

He was simply indispensable to the *Press*. Thus, powerful eyes averted when it came to his decision to destroy himself one Absolut bottle at a time. As long as he hit his numbers, Tom was free to operate in any way he saw fit. Sacking a book editor for drinking too much was akin to, as John Milius once wrote, "giving out speeding tickets at the Indianapolis 500."

Copy Chief hadn't forgotten about the old days. She'd been referred to as "Copy Chief" for so long—she ran the copy editing and production operations, thus the specificity of her title—that only three people in the company knew her real name. Jennifer Kensington. She, her own self, preferred to be addressed as Copy Chief. She never felt comfortable with Jennifer. As for her ex-husband Dick Kensington? The less said, the better.

Copy Chief employed many of the company's original story nerds who were now derogatorily referred to as "out-house" freelancers. They'd lost their "in-house" cubicles after a proclamation from the finance department just after the "2022 WeWork cash flow opportunity event." That's when *The People's Press LLC* bought out its floor space from the not-yet-profitable shared office space conglomerate.

The now isolated "out-housers" made their living wages through piecemeal projects Algernon's office parsed out with remarkable efficiency. Just when a valuable out-houser resolved to seek other sources of income, Copy Chief would be authorized to offer them a life-saving job to keep them afloat. It was uncanny how often that magic happened. It was almost as if Algernon had figured out each out-houser's financial breaking point.

Those in-house survivors of the budget cuts weren't much better off. Even Old Paint quietly admitted to Copy Chief that he was now contractually required to maintain a reasonable .09 or below blood alcohol content during regular business hours. He explained one evening to her, naturally over drinks, that his days in his forty-nine-square-foot cubicle had become an exercise in Vodka consumption management. He did all of his editing and acquiring in a two-hour burst just after his morning coffee/Leberkase. With tremens in remission, he'd clear his mind enough to maintain his ten-fold revenue contribution against his annual costs to the *Press*. His total cost came in at $289,750 per annum, which required a return of $2,897,500 of net revenue credited to his projects.

This quantifying of the creative editorial contribution to the bottom line was one of *The People's* industry-wide innovations, another game-changing Algernon invention. Now even the Big Five used the constantly updating report card for its employees.

The way it worked was that at any time an editor, copy editor, marketing person, and even the last vestiges of the sales department could check a company-mandated phone application, the app calculated the total money the employee contributed versus how expensive their position was to the Press. It was like one of those step counter apps that tell you how far you walked every day. Only for productivity. If you didn't hit your numbers consistently, your file would be "papered" until such time that you needed to transition "out of house." And once in the hinterlands, if you didn't measure up, the freelance life-sustaining work dried up. Extremely efficient.

But Old Paint was no idiot. After the App edict, he did the minimum viable work to justify his minimum viable pay. Not more. Not less. Why exceed expectations? Only chumps did that.

Copy Chief's *Slack* app buzzed with a mandatory message from "the tie-breaker's apprentice." An "all hands" meeting had just dropped into the schedule. She was to report to the Committee Room immediately for what was represented as "an exciting announcement."

The inner sanctum of the operation, the Committee Room, was highly secured.

After a nasty incident with Paul Pemberley, the former owner of the publishing house that became *The People's Press*, one could never be too vigilant. The CR also adjoined Pat Algernon's "sanctum sanctorum," an interconnecting maze of 144-square-footed cubicles that led to her corner operations office. The labyrinth was arranged to keep her systems engineers close at hand while safeguarding her from the "editorial talent."

Algernon was one of the core founding four who figured out the secret formula that allowed the minority shareholders of the former *Pemberley Press* to buy out the shares of its tyrannical founder. Power was money, and the core four, actually just one among them, had the money to seize the company away from Pemberley.

Pemberley was none too pleased about losing his Publisher's crown to a bunch of communists, so after an inadvisable number of old-fashioneds at the Century Club, he stormed the ramparts of the committee room to get satisfaction. But just as he pointed his bony finger at the upstarts, the oysters Rockefeller he'd had to add some foundation to his liquid courage repeated on him. All these years later, the room still smelled vaguely of low tide after Pemberley's unfortunate accident and his subsequent humiliation.

Not long after, the most intimidating of Algernon's revolutionary compatriots, the aforementioned Maria Harris Jones, decided to pursue, in the parlance of the standard sub-textual publicity release that softens the blow of being canned, "other opportunities." Fortunately, so the story goes, Algernon held down the fort even as *The People's Press* suffered a series of "terrible" performance years.

The official resurrection story of the *Press* was that even though the global worldwide readership was whittling down to a fraction of what it once was, under Algernon's leadership, the house was miraculously able to hold back the inevitable tide of dissolution. Cutbacks and sacrifices had to be made, of course, to accommodate the erosion of the readership base. But belt-tightening is the price of doing business, and the people of the *Press* hung together with aplomb.

Old Paint staggered down the hallway leading to the Committee room. Copy Chief waited for him outside, even allowing him to steady himself across the threshold by holding on to her shoulder.

"Excited assistants assuredly insist that this announcement is going to be sensational!" he slurred. Old Paint loved alliteration.

"Now, now, Old Paint. Let's not get cynical or lose our good cheer. Let's enjoy the camaraderie and being a part of the creative process..."

"Indeed, well put...forgive me, comrade."

"Gather round. Gather round!" Nigel Gefner whispered with a perfect mix of wink-wink irony to temper his seeming enthusiasm. A grandmaster mini-Machiavelli, Gefner maintained plausible deniability as his standard operating procedure. Should someone rise and dethrone Algernon, Gefner could quickly morph into their most needed and valued ally. Referencing his ironic gestures in the presence of the old leader, he'd claim that his support of the former figurehead was all a rouse until the rightful leader emerged. "The tie-breaker doesn't know we're in here...so shush..." Gefner always referred to Algernon as the "tie-breaker," never Pat or Algernon, or "the one who must be obeyed."

In the early days, *The People's Press* rejected the traditional structure that a single "publisher" or "editor-in-chief" make unilateral decisions about what the house would publish. Alternatively, as the original *raison d'etre* mission statement set forth, it clearly stated *that individual editors would instead bring their projects to a committee of colleagues.* The hive mind would then decide which projects to take to the marketplace and which ones to "pass" on. All other publishing personnel, including Copy Chief, were not included in these decisions, as they didn't have what is vaguely described as *editorial expertise.*

But after one too many controversial decisions by the committee (a hard pass on *The Da Vinciana Code* and the controversial approval of *Shark!* which, although highly profitable, was a critical laughing stock), a new approval process came online.

Algernon was recruited by all concerned to save the day. She became "the tie-breaker." The tie-breaker would have the last word on whether a project should be acquired. Algernon went to great lengths to show how uncomfortable the burden of responsibility made her to assume, and she'd reluctantly agreed to do so under the single condition that the sponsoring editor was given all of the credit for the success of the publication. She maintained she was an unsophisticated numbers person making a probability call. In no way did that qualify her as an "editor."

Not long after that, many projects became tied in the committee. And thus, Algernon was forced into making more and more decisions about the editorial direction of the company. She stoically did what had to be done.

Soon projects were announced at publication launch meetings that had never gone to committee, with the explanation that Algernon and the sponsoring editor had to make a quick decision on the project due to time constraints. You see, one of the Big Five houses was hot for the project, so *The People* had to strike quickly and decisively to ensure it would be a *People's* project.

Savvy editors, like Old Paint, understood that the eight-hour Wednesday committee meetings had now become pure theater. On those weekly intellectual Bataan Death marches, Gefner provisioned the troops with take-out. More often than not, the food comprised an eight-foot-long hoagie called "the big sandwich." It was his preferred choice as it was the cheapest option (watching the company pennies was rule number one for the assistant to the tie-breaker), and he always captured the least soggy wedge. Lunch was just after "the reading of the cards."

Of all of *The People's Press's* antiquated rituals, the reading of the cards was the most excruciating to experience. Gefner would stand at the head of the committee's oval conference table, by design not quite round, but not straight-edged either, and read a brief description of every single manuscript or proposal that had been submitted to the house the previous week. As there were now twelve full editors, plus twelve assistant editors and twenty-four editorial assistants, the volume of submissions astounded.

"Billick has in a memoir from Youtuber Rico, which reveals his personal struggles and triumphs overcoming the psychologically abusive relationship he had with his physical therapist just after he'd pulled his hamstring during his inimitable self-empowering removal of clothes demonstration on Spectrum Pay Per View Channel 769.

"Horvath has in a novel from Caitlin St. James, book eleven, entitled *The Return of Alfred* in her twenty-one-book epic set in the Gnome-iverse of little anthropomorphic beings dealing with big people problems."

And on and on. For fun, Old Paint made up submissions just to see if anyone in the room was paying attention.

Then, in the afternoon, when all of the editors' will was spent just staying upright listening to Gefner drone on, the laborious and painful process of groveling for acquisition money began.

Around the room, they'd go. Each editor got the floor to pitch the projects they wished to publish. Jensen would pitch his health book project. Sanchez would make a play for her postmodern literary pseudo-novel pastiche thing. Very predictable.

It was all very ecumenical, where no one seemed to have any particular advantage getting approval to offer an advance than anyone else. But the money at stake in these meetings was laughable. Hours would be spent hashing out the cost-benefit analysis of the tiniest project that warranted, at most, a $2,500 advance.

Old Paint had had enough success in his career picking winners (those projects he could buy cheaply and would then return a healthy contribution to his bottom line) that Algernon quietly gave him a budget to acquire whatever he wished as long as it did not exceed $25,000 advance per property. He took that as evidence of his superiority over the junior editors and made no secret about his special deal. It was enough power to keep him working on the farm without him considering he was being manipulated and exploited as keenly as were the up and coming young Turks beneath him.

And now they all stood in the committee room, desperately trying not to focus on Pemberley's old vomit stain still present in the northeast section of the wall-to-wall carpeting. Gefner, with his senses keen to the approach of authority, could make out Algernon striding down the hallway. He brought up his hands as a conductor would, and on cue, the semi-circle of lapdog editorial assistants began to sing to the tune of *For She's a Jolly Good Fellow*.

"The Tie-Breaker is Number One.

The Tie-Breaker is Number One.

Which Nobody Can Deny

And Number Ones Should Be in Private!
And Number Ones Should Be in Private!
And Number Ones Should Be in Private!
Which Nobody Can Deny."

Copy Chief arched an eyebrow at Old Paint, who returned his best "I don't know what the fuck is going on either" expression back at her.

Algernon graced them with her presence and was all smiles as Gefner calmed the chorus and turned to make his announcement.

"I'm pleased to announce that *The People's Press* has added an extra restroom to the floor!"

It was true that doing what one had to do inside of the People's poorly ventilated and yet acoustically dynamic loo was not a pleasant experience. But as another of the *raison d'etre* mission statement principles clearly stated, "We're all in this together," it just wasn't cricket to complain.

So, one made accommodations. Copy Chief usually took a "morning contemplation walk" that led to the Four Seasons Hotel and did her business in the more civilized private quarters within the Hotel's Nobu franchise facilities.

Now, to have another bathroom on the floor was almost too good to be true.

Like a pied piper, Gefner led the group into Algernon's corner "cubicle" and opened one of her storage closet doors. Inside was a pristine bathroom with not just a perfectly proportioned toilet but a private shower with a double marble-topped sink too. It was a Valhalla of elimination.

He then opened up an official-looking document that had *The People's* seal and signatures from all of its board of directors...whoever they were.

"In appreciation for our record performance on *The New York Sun's Bestseller* list, we the shareholders and People of the *Press* acknowledge and applaud the selfless and tireless work of our tiebreaker, Pat Algernon," Gefner teared up just a bit at the end.

It was true that *The People's* winter season had proved remarkably sizzling. *The People's Press* now held the top four fiction slots and three of the top ten in nonfiction too on *The New York Sun's* list. The entire office had been giddy for weeks.

The only ones not encouraged by the sizzling start to the year were Old Paint and Copy Chief. They knew about the soft underbelly of the company and were concerned that as Old Paint drunkenly put it, "The People have shot their wad." The company did not have many revenue-producing titles left in its coffers for the rest of the year. The fact too was that it was only March 23.

"Theirs not to reason why. Theirs but to do or die," said Copy Chief whenever Old Paint kvetched about it.

And after the traditional thin slice of Duane Reade sheet cake and another nod from Gefner, the in-house staff filed out with their "to-go" clementine (the tie-breaker's favorite fruit) to enjoy back at their desks.

Old Paint followed Copy Chief back to her cubicle. He jerked his head toward the elevators as he shuffled past. Fifteen minutes later, they met in the building's lobby eighteen floors below.

"Des will let us in the back door at *Langan's*. I need a black and tan to take the edge off..."

But Copy Chief stayed put.

"Come on, Chief, it ain't worth another thought... Seeing through the game ain't the same as winning the game. Am I right?"

Copy Chief nodded behind Old Paint, gesturing to the twenty-foot by forty-foot LCD screen behind him. "Notice anything different?"

The core four of *The People's Press* had spent endless hours just after the Pemberley takeover to come up with a simple single tagline to express the authentic ethos of their new vision for a publishing house. Featherton, the real poet of the movement and the woman who'd spent all of her inherited wealth buying up Pemberley shares on the black market, finally encapsulated the "why" of their new venture.

THE WORK ABOVE ALL ELSE

It was a potent message.

So potent that multimillion-copy bestseller Steven Prince left *Leviathan Publishing* to come to *The People's Press* six months after the company's rebranding. He was enchanted by the idea of the place and convinced it was a publishing house conducive to helping him level up his skills. Plus, he would also get fresh street credibility to reach a new, younger breed of readers.

His press announcement called it an inclusive publishing house that put the art above the artist. Prince commented, "When I heard that phrase, THE WORK ABOVE ALL ELSE, I knew it was the place for me. Any real writer knows that once the work is done, once it's in the world, the writer has no real claim on it anymore. It's like a child. The only thing that keeps me working is the work, trying to get a little better with each project. I just had to be a part of this new thing."

Old Paint didn't know why Copy Chief stood so stunned. The tagline looked to him as it ever did.

"Look closer." Copy Chief was nothing if not meticulous. She once stopped a press because of a misplaced umlaut on the Hungarian translation of Prince's *The Standing*, *The People's* first million-copy print run.

"Nope, still don't see it."

"Look at each word, letter by letter. Remember that old *Twilight Zone* episode, 'To Serve Man'? Take your time, read it, and think about it!"

Old Paint focused again. The scroll came back around, and this time, he made out what had caused Copy Chief to stiffen and shudder.

THE WORKERS ABOVE ALL ELSE

"Fuck me...yep, that's some edit. It's now the exact opposite of what we originally intended. Three letters and the entire meaning flip-flops."

Des, as always, gave Old Paint and Copy Chief a hearty hug inside *Langan's* kitchen door. He even stepped behind the bar himself to tap their first round. A few later, Copy Chief and Old Paint had tucked the new slogan deep into the recesses of their minds.

In the weeks that followed, Pat Algernon became a fixture at the *Four Seasons*. Her morning breakfasts turned into grill room lunches, which morphed into evening pool party events. So much so that Copy Chief, unable to bear the incessant Algernon face time, had to abandon her favorite stall at Nobu. It was simply not conducive to her health. Des gave her a key to *Langan's* back door so she could use the facilities in peace. He kept a nice bottle of slivovitz on the counter with a small glass for her too. She found the plum brandy perfect for settling her increasingly sensitive stomach.

Things could be worse, she kept telling herself.

Old Paint maintained a calm disposition and managed to break out yet another writer onto *The New York Sun's Bestseller* list. And not coincidentally, as a result, the expense account receipts that accounting had been demanding from him for months were now no longer necessary to produce. Algernon herself texted him that she was so pleased she'd upped his allowable in-office blood alcohol limit to .11, which he quickly tabulated amounted to another two ounces of Vodka per hour.

Old Paint knew the score. It was an old tune.

Every time he heard from accounting about his monthly *Langan's* bills, he knew he had to go out and dig up another bestseller. The man was nothing if not resilient. He now singlehandedly accounted for 37 percent of *The People's Press'* annual gross revenue while his salary and benefits cost 2.52 percent. But he had a lovely split-level home in Harrison. His daughter just graduated from Harvard, and his wife had made peace with what he liked to refer to as his alternative lifestyle. Things could definitely be worse.

Nigel Gefner now headed up *The People's* Synergy department, looking for movie tie-in projects and breaking bread with the

Oops.

SOCIETY

thought leaders in the industry to see how one might stretch the company dollars even further. Under his onus, Peter Wile from *Infinitum House* and reps from the other four big fives got the grand tour to see if there might be some industry-wide innovations to conjure together. How might they make that year's depressing 1.3 percent revenue increase across the industry even higher?

Gefner explained that the cubicle "open office" system had reduced the floor footprint for the company to a minimum viable in-house accommodation. He added that non-essential personnel had been transitioned outside of house where the overhead would not be *The People's* responsibility.

Wile nodded with appreciation, "Say, young man, could you give me the code for the private loo?"

On Thursday nights, the editor of *The New York Sun's Book Review* ranked the next week's bestsellers and then sent her list for the following Sunday out to "all concerned." To get on that email list required the purchase of advertising space in the skimpy weekly pamphlet. *The People's Press* didn't advertise for years until Stephen Prince joined their stable. Then it "had to." His agent has insisted that alerting the accounts and the readers of the book review that Prince had churned out yet another irresistible bestseller for them to consume be in the contract.

They hadn't stopped advertising since, even sponsoring a cheeky cover that Copy Chief and Old Paint had cooked up as an April Fool's Day prank. It was filled with hilarious fake insider stories about the business, comparing the most respected literary editor in the industry to Mephistopheles. It was the talk of the town for months, even though not a single person told Old Paint or Copy Chief they'd enjoyed it, except for the stuffy editor they'd parodied. He called Old Paint to say, "I thought it was marvelous."

That's just how it was. Praise was only parceled out to the pathetic—those on the slippery slope destined to freelance-hood—to keep their chins up before their inevitable fall. The real pros only took a ribbing for their failures...never were they backslapped for their triumphs. And when they did get a kind word, it made them paranoid because chances were they were in for a sacking.

Old Paint had a marginally better bottle in his drawer for Thursday nights. And later, after the scorecard came in and he'd pre-gamed at the office, he would celebrate or console himself with double Stolis with just a squinch of soda with lime at *Langan's* with Des.

Tonight, though, he was desperate for Jay Pincher's latest to debut at #1. His summer vacation rental depended on it as he received a bonus every time one of his authors hit #1...just enough for his two weeks in Wellfleet in August.

As he contemplated summer Sunday flea market finds of yesteryear, he heard the distracting ping signaling a new email. Old Paint said a hail Mary, threw back the dregs of his lukewarm Vodka and clicked through.

It wasn't the list. It was a breaking story for those who'd been tagged by the newspaper's bots for its "book publishing interest" portal.

INFINITUM HOUSE BUYS NICHE PUBLISHER

And then another ping. Old Paint clicked that one too.

"Aha!"

Pincher was #1 with a monster first-week performance. Old Paint was now definitely on his way to Wellfleet, and after checking his "Contribution App," he was now fifteen times above his cost.

He resolved that the best course of action was a huge blowout expense dinner at 21. He'd begin with the shrimp cocktail, follow up with the Dover sole, and top it off with baked Alaska. He texted Copy Chief to meet him at the front of the restaurant for the celebration. She was the only one he cared to share his good fortune with . Plus, she would steady him into the building. The stairs into that place were a nightmare when you were well lubricated. He gave himself a black eye the last time he tried to negotiate them by himself.

D'Artagnon, the Maître D, took their coats. He congratulated them on the Pincher performance and, with a wink, escorted them into a private dining room. It was off of a side door near the kitchen.

"Mr. Dachson...I just love the new Pincher. As a token of my appreciation, I thought I might return a little entertainment to you." He then went to the opposite wall and pulled back the beautiful tapestry that adorned it.

Old Paint and Copy Chief ducked.

"Not to worry...not to worry, my friends. They can't see you. This is a one-way mirror we use to evaluate the performance of the staff during private parties. We can come back here and watch and listen to the service without disturbing the patrons. We can see them, but they can't see us. Like a cop show." With that, he went to the opposite side of the room and turned a dial. Now Old Paint and Copy Chief could hear as well as see what was transpiring on the other side of the wall.

Through the looking glass sat *Infinitum House's* CEO Peter Wile, Pat Algernon, Gefner, and a whole slew of conservatively dressed men and women having dinner. The mood was jovial.

Old Paint now remembered the first email he got from *The New York Sun*. He clicked through his cell phone to find it again.

INFINITUM HOUSE BUYS NICHE PUBLISHER

March 23, 2027
New York, NY

Austrian media conglomerate, Infinitum Zarathustra LLP, has acquired *The People's Press*, formerly *Pemberley Publishing*, for an undisclosed sum. It brings what one book publishing insider describes as "the best of both worlds" under one roof. I Zarathustra's global assets include printing facilities across the seven continents (the Antarctic facility having come online last quarter) as well as artificially intelligent copy editing, proofreading, interior design, and cover design services. The largest Publisher in the world with annual revenues of 21.67 billion in 2026, it assumes all titles under copyright at *The People's Press* including international bestseller wunderkind Melissa Ford's first novel *Fulcrum's Apotheosis*, which last quarter became the bestselling title of the century, generating an estimated 1.7 billion in profits and rumored to have been the engine by which *The People's Press* quietly bought up its outstanding shares.

Peter Wile, CEO of *Infinitum House*, US called the acquisition "the jewel in the crown of his administration," while *The People's Press* "Tie-Breaker" Pat Algernon had this to say: "We've always put our story workers above all else, and to bring them into the resource-rich and powerful systems inherent within Infinitum was a no-brainer. In the coming months, after a short leave of absence to tend to some personal matters, I'm looking forward to working with Peter and his team to sort out the careful restructuring necessary to meld our two cultures. This is a great day for *The People!*"

They were celebrating the acquisition. And Old Paint and Copy Chief had a front-row seat to the bacchanalia.

D'Artagnon mixed them highballs and then took their orders. He then quietly closed the door behind him.

Wile rose as his supporting salary-people struck the tines of their forks against 21's finest crystal.

"Comrades..." all chuckled politely, "...may I propose a toast to the newest members of the Infinitum family. Before I do, though, I'd just like to set the record straight." Some uncomfortable chair shifting ensued. "As you all know, my dear chum from school, both Hotchkiss and Yale, in fact, is Paul Pemberley."

The party hushed, all attention was now centered on Wile.

"Where's he going with this?" asked Copy Chief of Old Paint.

"Shit...this is going to be good!" Old Paint reached for the volume dial and turned it up.

"And when our honored guests tonight, especially Pat Algernon, deftly maneuvered a majority of Pemberley's shareholders into supporting their vision for a new kind of publishing concern...I was, to put it indecorously, gob smacked. But upon further reflection, I was not overly concerned. We all find ourselves, at one point in our career or another, at the mercy of market forces. Paul, while brilliant, was no exception.

"He unadvisedly took his hand off of the controls at his place. He let the creatives, the editors, and their ilk, out of their tightly sealed sandbox. Pemberley opened up the books to them, gave them too much leeway, too much information about how this business really works, about how the frontlist is a smokescreen for the annual return of the backlist of titles we've owned and controlled for centuries. Pemberley's ouster was the inevitable result. No, it wasn't Paul's fall that concerned me.

"It was the idea that a company run by a bunch of creatives could ever reach profitability. I suspected that with such touchy-feely personalities at the helm, it would soon hemorrhage so much money I'd be able to buy up the Pemberley backlist for pennies on the dollar. After all, I reasoned, editors are ignorant of the ebb and flow of commerce. Best to keep them that way. Let's let events take their course, I resolved." He paused for effect and took a sip of water before continuing.

"Much to my utter shock, though, this new company, what was rechristened *The People's Press* for goodness' sake...ruthlessly built itself over just these past twelve years into a mini-major. And when we reviewed their accounts? I was astonished! Their overhead is 18 percent beneath ours. Their employee benefits 48 percent less taxing on the bottom line than ours. And they've had an average return on investment of 17 percent per year! In our best years, we'll crack a hair over 15. Obviously, Pat and her team have a secret sauce! And I have no intention of letting a secret sauce remain untasted. Best to ask for the recipe, with the appropriate financial incentives, of course..." Chuckles all around.

"So let us all raise our glasses to the remarkable architect of the new publishing paradigm, where keeping the workers above all else in line is the core concentration...Pat Algernon." All drank a deep quaff.

Wile began to take his seat again but then decided he had one more thing to offer.

"If I may be so bold as to share one more story with this group. In our research, one of our *bots* came back with the derivation of the name Algernon. Apparently, it derives from the Norman-French meaning 'with mustaches.' And as I'm sure *The People's Press* team discovered during its due diligence, our code name for the operation was Operation Mustache Pat in homage to the masterminds of the Sicilian underworld, the Mustache Petes."

Pat smiled, but no one was quite sure what kind of smile it was.

"It was in all due respect for your talents, Pat. To build a powerbase from nothing as you did is astonishing just as *La Cosa Nostra* was an astonishing success for Italian Americans." With that, Wile, at last, relinquished the floor.

The applause was sincere and well sustained.

Algernon rose at just the right time to offer her response. Old Paint and Copy Chief hadn't touched their Dover sole, so D'Artagnon brought in a steam bath contraption to keep it from drying out. The show was both mesmerizing and horrifying to take in, like watching a slow-motion train wreck while also being a passenger.

"Thank you, Peter. Can I just say how thrilled we all are to be here. To be welcomed so eloquently into, let's face it, the only real publishing operation today. We who live in the shadow of your 653 imprints, your global distribution networks and your deep acquisition coffers can only pinch ourselves that we've been recognized as worthy of joining your establishment, which has outlasted all others in creative enterprises. Music, movies, all fallen idol marketplaces have been disrupted beyond recognition. Only books remain intact. No matter, Jeff Bezos. The powers that be in book publishing are the same as they've ever been. But if I do say so myself, we do have some secret sauces we can share to improve your, I mean *our*, bottom line. In that spirit, I'll offer one potent but straightforward principle tonight."

It was now her turn to take a sip of water.

"Never underestimate the power of language. Editors, for all of their creative insights, are as children. They crumble when confronted with the right language. Let's walk through it.

"Number one, the writer gets cover credit. Number two, the writer gets a chunk of the revenue, even if I think we need to revisit just how much." The tinkle of forks hitting glasses again.

"But what does the editor get from the creative process? And don't kid yourselves, the best editors put their souls into these books. What do they get other than the personal satisfaction of fixing the dross that writers deliver and the satisfaction of making it 'work'? The answer? Not much. They get a bottle of booze and a slap on the back. Is that enough? I say it is more than enough. What editors really want is our approval, our respect, our appreciation—we, the owners of the machinery that sells their precious titles. So much so that they're willing to accept: number one, the meager salaries we offer and number two, the complete lack of job security. All for the price of the slightest verbal attaboy or a metaphorical pat on the head. So, what's my advice? Keep the pats to a minimum but withhold them at your peril. That is how to keep your editors' noses to the grindstone. That has been our company's overriding management policy since I took it over...to focus on THE WORKERS ABOVE ALL ELSE."

A hearty round of applause followed. A genuine expression of awe was on Peter Wile's face. He'd have to keep a close eye on this one. Thankfully the twenty-five million he'd ponied up to buy her "B" series shares had already been approved in Vienna. She would fade away as all of the others had. Give her this moment, he thought. It will be her last.

"But I do take issue with one small detail," Pat continued.

"I do apologize for that Mustache Pat reference," chimed in Wile.

"On no, not that...I actually love that, Peter." More laughs. "It is simply our desire that *The People's Press* return to our roots. To our traditions. To honor the backlist of titles that we inherited all those years ago. If I may, I'd like to bring in a special guest."

The room hushed.

Algernon motioned to the entryway.

Old Paint and Copy Chief on the other side of the glass sat catatonic. For there, in the entryway stood Paul Pemberley, the former owner and publisher of *Pemberley Publishing*. The private diners had all risen in unison with thunderous applause. Seeing his dear old Bearcat Bunkie and fellow Skull and Bones-ian so dapperly leaning against the door jam, Wile dabbed tears from his eyes with his phi-beta-kappa pocket square.

Algernon, sensing the perfect amount of time for all to be bedazzled by her introduction, continued.

"It is with great pleasure that I announce that Mr. Paul Pemberley has graciously agreed to serve as the executive chairman of our little operation within Infinitum Zarathustra from here on in. And I relied heavily upon his counsel in our negotiations."

"Now, I know why we had to pay two times earnings instead of the standard 1.2!" Wile shouted.

Pemberley at last spoke. "Dear Wile, the backlist is worth four times. You received the accommodation."

"True! Very True!" Wile laughed as he lunged out of his seat and embraced his old chum.

"Now, boys, please let me finish," said Algernon.

"Yes, sorry, mother..." the men pretended to take their scolding to the delighted audience.

"Now then. With Paul serving on our executive board and our mutually agreed intention to revisit and refresh the neglected Pemberley backlist, we believe it is in the best interests of all to kick off a new iteration of our company. We will change the name of *The People's Press* to..."

At this moment the lights dimmed and the utterly deferential 21 staff entered with a large Bouley Bakery sheet cake decorated as such:

P⁴ PUBLISHING
THE BEST OF BOTH WORLDS

"To Piss to the Fourth Power Publishing." Old Paint sloshed up his glass, but could not manage to rise to the occasion.

But Copy Chief was too stunned to take up the toast.

A half-hour later, after they'd rallied and eaten the sole and baked Alaska, both were properly pissed themselves as they watched the last throes of the celebration through the one-way glass. The revelers were now engaged in an old Russian vodka drink-off game, which Wile liked to play to remind everyone of his murky Moscow past.

It wasn't much of a game, really. No skill necessary. Just a stupid contest to see who could drink more before passing out. Truth be told, it was straight out of one of the opening scenes of *Raiders of the Lost Ark*.

Jesus didn't anyone do anything original anymore, Copy Chief thought.

Wile and Algernon were the contestants, and from the looks of it, both were very close to face-planting. Each had six shot glasses turned over on his and her side of the table.

And then the room took on an ominous tone.

A suddenly suspicious Algernon grabbed Wile's bottle and took a deep drink.

"He's put water in here!" she screamed, but just as she shouted her accusation, Wile grabbed her bottle and drank.

"Looks like you've done the same thing!" Wile shouted.

STATUS

THE GOOD DAUGHTER

Written by Rachelle Ramirez
Edited by Anne Hawley

I'm washing dishes when you call. "Sharlene, you didn't call me back with your mother's intake information."

"Sorry," I say. I dropped Mom at her apartment across town and rushed home to make cereal and eggs for dinner. There wasn't time to make anything else after Zac's dentist appointment and Connor's school play that—

Zac tugs on my pants leg. "Can you play with us now?"

I look down, "Sorry, Zac, I—"

Zac rolls his eyes. "You promised."

I crouch to his level. "Honey, go ask Connor to help you set up the Mario game in the basement, okay?"

Zac trudges toward the basement door.

"Sorry," I tell him. "I need to do this for your Nana, and I—"

You interrupt. You are doing us a tremendous favor. You have a state-of-the-art treatment facility and an Ivy League treatment team. You need a Collateral Contact Interview.

Collateral contact? What you mean is someone close to the patient, someone responsible for their care. There is no one else you can call. My sisters made lives on the other side of the country just so caregivers wouldn't call and so Mom wouldn't call in the middle of the night because she lost her keys or money or mind.

You are certain you can teach me the skills I need to help her recover.

I put you on speaker phone, and your words, like my hands, swirl into the sudsy gray dishwater.

An unbreakable Corelle bowl slips from my greasy hands, hits the sink, and cracks down the center.

"Shit!" A few blood drops hit the water from my thumb. "I have to put you on hold for a sec." I drop the bowl in the trash, leaving me with an uneven number of dishes and no way of replacing it since the pattern was discontinued. They were a wedding gift, now as disintegrated as my marriage. I tight-wrap my thumb in a paper towel.

You insist I bring Mom in for an appointment tomorrow, something about recovery.

"It's not like I'm hanging out at the beach all day!"

Connor hollers up from the basement. "Mom, don't start yelling."

"I'm not yelling!"

I bite my tongue so I can do the right thing and be a good person. I can get her to her appointments. I'm not a total idiot. But she doesn't want me to babysit her twenty-four-seven, doesn't want me cleaning up after her when she's so out of it that she pisses on my two-hundred-dollar Ikea rug. I clench my teeth so the words don't come out. "I just wish—" Shut up, Sharlene. "I wish she'd die already." Shit.

You rustle papers, maybe trying to contain your remark, perhaps looking in your copy of the Diagnostic and Statistical Manual for answers. You tell me how I don't mean what I say.

She made her choices and cut corners to nubs, despite her stories of how hard she worked as a mother, how many sacrifices she made, blah, blah, blah. Either I drowned those memories in gallons of ice cream, or she concocts those stories.

You want me to say more about that and speak to her strengths. Everything I did and didn't do throbs in my bleeding thumb—the weak, hopeless tiny moments of living—the mistakes. Collateral person.

I dry dishes with a towel. You want her history.

"I don't know. Mom was born just short of four pounds, and Grandma swears she did everything just exactly right." Racked with guilt, Grandma would say, "I bought the best formula as soon as her crazy-ass father got that great job as a machinist. They didn't have books back then on parenting. No instruction manuals like your spoiled generation has."

"Mom was beautiful, you know? Young and fast." Too fast. If you look at her black and white childhood pictures, she's in color—pinched-pink cheeks and crystal blue eyes, everyone else in dishwater gray and black. When I used to look at the pictures of her younger than six, I wished I could whisk back in time and snatch her away before the abuse started, before Grandma married Clyde. Look at the pictures of her after age seven and anyone can see the difference. But apparently, Grandma was blinded by her devotion to Clyde just as she was by her reliance on all the Johns that passed through after he left. Grandma insisted it was all Mom's bullshit, that Mom was jealous of her relationship with Clyde. But Grandma's eyes tell a different story—one where Mom was the sacrifice to keep Clyde around, at least until Mom squealed and Clyde was taken into custody. Grandma still blames her for that.

You yammer about triggering incidents and mental illness and a possible bright side to the disease, which is your own pile of bullshit.

I peek in on Zac and Connor in the basement and find them agreeing to another Mario game in hopes of postponing bedtime.

You finally pause. Maybe you realize you're a bore? You try again to get me to talk about her strengths.

She told fantastical stories about being a concert pianist, about winning state gymnastics competitions, about turning down a "full ride to brain surgeon school." She loved the fizz of Pepsi, and the staleness of peanut brittle. She got such a tickle out of her waterbed sloshing around every time she climbed in for another all-day-long nap. She said she could read people's minds, but we couldn't get her to go and play a game of high-stakes poker to make the rent.

I know your time is valuable and billable, and it's after hours and your rates are up, so you don't have to explain what bipolar is. I'm almost thirty and I've spent a lifetime under its grisly paw.

I pull the broken Corelle bowl out the trash and try Super Gluing it together. "Sometimes, she was so fragile and dark." I had to carry her emotions with me, had to dole them out and tell her what to feel so she would feel anything at all. I tried keeping only happy feelings and giving them to her like Lemonhead candies, but they always soured when she tasted them.

You say she reports no suicide events and this is promising.

I say, "Define event. Not successful at least."

You are apparently waiting for my elaboration.

"I was sure it was all my fault," I say. "When I was ten, Mom was out of it, and I tried to make dinner, but I burned the mac-n-cheese. Smoke filled the house, and my sisters and I couldn't get Mom out of bed. The neighbor called the firemen who rushed in and pulled Mom out, unconscious." I'd really done it that time. I'd killed her. But then she resurrected like Jesus on the third day and walked out of the ICU full of acidic blood and words. "She needed 'kidney treatments,' and I owed it to her to take her on the 45 bus and read *People Magazine* to her while she was hooked up to the hateful machine." Assuming the nurses and techs blamed me for her suffering, I kept my head down in repentance.

You want to know what else I can tell you.

"That Super Glue sucks. I'm trying to fix a bowl and the freakin' bowl is determined to stay broken. You think it will set with time?"

"I don't know about repairing things," you say.

I laugh, but you fail to see the irony. I secure the bowl with a rubber band and plunge my hands back in the dishwater—a task I can actually manage.

You tell me it's never too late to invest in her more and to tell her I love her and that I believe she will get better. "These are acts of compassion," you say. "Real compassion. And who better to do it?"

I let that sink in as you rustle those papers.

You point out that she is in financial trouble and that I've been unable to help financially.

"I try. Do you know of any agencies that reimburse for phone bills, transportation, in-home follow-ups, anything?"

You don't know. Aha! Another something you don't know. None of you people know the answers to that one.

You point out that my mom can count on me for reliable transportation.

"Yeah, like when I had to take her to the ER with 'scratches' on her wrists in a taxi that cost two days' wages. They agreed to keep her." I walked home with the sounds of car horns and 'Hey Baby' and 'How much?' The answer ringing through me was, 'Not much. Not much at all.' Once home, I turned Def Leppard on high volume until a counselor like you called.

After an hour-long discussion of my mother's "limited options," I learned that the smoke all those years ago hadn't hurt Mom at all. She'd overdosed on three bottles of Tylenol long before the water boiled out of the mac-n-cheese. Then, somehow, I couldn't make myself go and see her on visitation days. I started college again and fell for Travis, the first guy who said I was pretty and stuck around the next day.

"When Mom finally came home on her new medications, she was slow." So slow and gray. She couldn't balance on her waterbed and drained it out onto the bedroom carpet. "I got her into a day rehab program." Even though I'd heard it was a shitty place, it was the only one that would take her. It was the only way I could keep my new second job at Burger King, and the counselor from the hospital said it was for the best that I do less. I liked that counselor well enough but I felt like I was betraying Mom. "Soon Mom refused to go to the day program." She had her reasons: Oprah's guest that day was a celebrity she loved, the cat was sick, it might snow in August.

"And you let her stay home and deteriorate?"

"I tried to get her to go, but she'd just say, 'I didn't raise you as smart as I thought if you don't see that beer works better than art projects and bingo.'"

You say I enabled her.

"What could I do? I was pregnant with Connor, so I married Travis." I didn't know Travis had all those girlfriends. I was a stupid bride. "Mom wore a jester costume to the wedding."

You chuckle.

But she bought a few Corelle dishes from the registry, maybe even this damn bowl, and I figured that was blessing enough. It wasn't long before Mom tossed her meds in the trash and went down fast. I missed my final exams that week, too afraid to leave Mom alone. I hid the steak and butter knives and then realized she could hang herself with a bedsheet or a shoelace or just step in front of the 72 bus as it barreled past the house. Even if I dismantled the house, she'd need babysitting. She hates it when I call it babysitting. Connor was born with complications. There wasn't time to discuss.

I stack the last dish to dry. Connor and Zac are arguing over the Mario mushroom car and who gets to use the better controller.

"Mom's doctor convinced me to have her committed to the psych ward." I couldn't or wouldn't visit her as I promised. Life got super busy. Travis was working and gone all the time, and they didn't allow babies on the ward. I soon got the call that she was stealing from other patients. She would be kept in "a private suite with room service and a view of the garden." Later, I learned it was solitary confinement. Finally, she agreed to take the medications. She swore she was better. She should go home.

She started receiving disability checks and could finally afford to go to a bar, which meant a new snaggletoothed boyfriend eventually trailed her home. She loved him to his rotten bones. She kept him supplied with Coors Light and Cablevision, and he promised never to leave. Until one day he did.

Connor and I even stayed at Mom's house on some of her terrored nights, hoping to haul her into The Program in the morning. I'd climb into her bed when she had nightmares and she'd put her head on my enormous pregnant belly and beg the baby to be a girl. "Don't grow a penis," she would say. "Penises are bad." But there was Connor and all his appointments, nap schedules, and feedings. I was pregnant with Zac and busy following Travis around and trying to prove to myself he wasn't cheating—or that he was.

You have more to say.

"Somehow we held it together for a couple of torrid years." Then Mom started showing up at our house to hug Connor, just to see her "angel." Connor loved his Grandma who laughed loudly and played hard. He had no idea she was shit-faced as she raced Matchbox cars and crashed them into the wall.

Mom's number appears on my caller ID. I put you on hold and check the other line. It could be an emergency.

Mom is happy or drunk or both, and she remembers she has an intake tomorrow at the new clinic in the burbs. "Maybe they won't be dumbasses and will find a medicine that works," she says. "What are you up to, burning dinner?"

Funny. This is my nighttime routine. Dishes. Baths. Packing lunchboxes and backpacks." Your intake counselor from the clinic is on the other line." I yell toward the basement for the boys to get their pajamas on and brush their teeth.

"You do too much," she says. "I can help with the kitchen stuff, you know. I can at least do better than that idiot Travis ever could."

"It's too late for me to come and get you and you know you won't. Just yesterday, you wanted my help with your kitchen."

"It doesn't matter anyway," Mom says. "I'll be dead soon enough. Can't take this much longer."

I refuse her trap. "I'm about to read the boys the baseball book you bought. And be ready when I show up at noon tomorrow. I don't want to spend an hour this time looking for a missing shoe. And—Mom." I take a deep breath. What did the counselor tell me to say? "I know you can get better. You can do this because you're strong, and..."

"Feed that horse shit to someone else. Be here by noon, or I'll be the one faking the smile. You wanna help me for real? Bring a bottle of Smirnoff, the good stuff, not the cheap crap." She hangs up.

I swallow back a sigh and tap back to you, dear counselor. "You were explaining something? I'm sorry. Things are hectic." I need to get the kids to bed. Connor needs his night medication. My mother's care is not a task like washing dishes. I need a proper Band-Aid and Neosporin for my thumb. "Forgive me for letting you go?"

"Sharlene, we'll see you tomorrow afternoon?"

I hang up.

I grab the glue clotted bowl and drop it in the trash, rubber band and all.

I find Connor and Zac rummaging through the laundry room for pajamas. I help Connor find his Batman favorites in the dryer.

I sit on the bottom bunk in the boys' room to tuck Zac in.

"Mom, will you play soccer with us tomorrow since you didn't today?" Zac asks.

Connor climbs to the top bunk. "She can't 'cause she's taking Nana somewhere again tomorrow."

I get up and turn on the nightlight. "How about tomorrow we let your Nana do things her way and the three us play hooky at the beach?"

MORALITY

AN ARTIST'S TEST

Written by Kimberly Kessler
Edited by Abigail K. Perry

Everyone knows at least one in their life—that person who sees beauty in the tired mundane of the everyday, the quintessential artist. Laura was just such a person.

Through her eyes, tire tracks in mud would transform into delicate patterns on paned glass. A yard of dandelion weeds grew into a golden forest for bees. The void of a broken window became a sunburst. Her artist's eyes and deft fingers were like living antennae, absorbing the energy of potential around her and then weaving it back in delicious and meticulous detail, often with whatever medium was nearby.

While they were dating, Eric would invite her over for dinner and Laura would offer to set the table. He'd turn around from his skillet of chicken curry to find her folding disposable napkins like origami masterpieces or building a bud vase of fresh flowers from an empty olive oil bottle. Even the angle of his worn-out utensils on his mismatched dishes would appear charming and original. Like magic.

All her life, Laura gave custom gifts: hand-beaded earrings, a re-finished end table, stationery stamped with an original poem. When-ever Eric took her to a party, she'd sip wine and sketch portraits from a cozy corner. He would work the room, chatting easily and sending secret smiles her way. Even her grocery lists shined—wide-ruled mas-terpieces adorned with cursive script and shaded drawings of egg-plant and Eggo waffles. In all her subtle and special ways, she used her Midas touch to make the world around her beautiful.

· · · · · ·

It's the end of her shift. Laura's feet ache at the register, and the humming fluorescent lights make the space behind her eyes throb. The floor manager puts the "this lane is closed" sign at her station. She sings a silent hallelujah and stomachs her way through one more smile, receipt, and "Thank you for shopping at Walmart" before spinning the platform of plastic bags with a flourish. She clocks out. Hoists herself into the truck, and locks the blue lan-yard and employee badge in the glove box.

Until tomorrow.

It's just a quick drive to pick up her two sons from their grand-mother's. She parks in the driveway and says a silent prayer that her mother-in-law will refrain from criticizing her about the boys' unkempt hair. Not that it makes any difference. She has no choice but to endure her. With Eric gone three years, her sister off travel-ing the world, and her own mother remarried (again) and moved to Arizona, Sofia is the only support around to help. And as much as she hates it, she'd be lost without her.

Laura manages to shoo the boys out to the truck quickly, blaming her raging headache for not wanting to stay for dinner. She avoids any small talk. But in the truck, while thirteen-year-old Den stares silently out the window, ten-year-old Jax chatters non-stop. Laura nods along, remarking, "Mmm, that's cool," at regular intervals. Her gaze flits from the rearview mirror to the dashboard clock. Only three hours until bedtime.

Once home, the boys rush past her. They dump their bags in the entryway and head upstairs, no doubt hoping to gorge on video games before dinner. Laura's easel stands lonesome in the corner as a half-completed painting pouts at her. Irritated. She returns the look, aching to disappear into strokes of color against canvas. To disappear into anything. Disappear altogether. To not have to think about anyone else's needs but her own.

She walks to the easel and runs her fingers over the bumpy texture. The first layer of blue sky and green fields are long since dry. She eyes the tray of oils neatly arranged on the table beside it, undisturbed and gathering dust. She rubs the bristles of a brush between her fingers. Surely the boys wouldn't mind not eating until later. They need downtime, too.

"Mom? What's for dinner?"

Her next inhale is deliberate and she turns away from the canvas and back to the kitchen. She plops her purse on the counter and sets a pot of water on the stove. With the burner turned high, she adds a few dashes of salt and kisses the remnants from her fingertips. Like he would have.

Now it's just a waiting game.

She calls the boys back to the table, knowing full well they didn't finish their homework at Grandma's. They moan and groan like she's canceled Christmas but nevertheless comply. Jax practices his spelling words aloud, like he's auditioning for bloody Broadway. Den scribbles on his algebra sheet, silently as usual. Laura watches him out of the corner of her eye as she readies a package of spaghetti and wonders if his brooding lately is just a phase or something else. Something worse. But part of her is just grateful that at least one aspect of her life isn't asking for more of her.

As the water finally boils, she adds the stiff noodles, breaking them in half and then squashing them down with a fork to submerge them. She caps it with a lid and then pulls another pan from the cupboard, passively pouring in a jar of her mother-in-law's homemade sauce. Eric always made their sauce from scratch. Mealtime was the most magical time of the day with Eric home. For one, she never had to cook. She would sketch at the counter while Eric entertained her with his commentary. Every ingredient came with a story or a song, told or sung in the accent befitting its origins. Then he would bring the spoon to her lips for her to test it. He wasn't satisfied until it was so delicious she couldn't take a bite without closing her eyes. That was his cue. His victory. He'd huzzah and kiss her neck before returning to his skillet.

She stares into the pan of red, letting her gaze phase out of focus and longing for another place and time.

"Treachery."

"What?" She resurfaces and looks at her younger son.

"Treachery. T-R-E-A-C-H-E-R-Y. Treachery. Did I get it right?"

She nods, smiling encouragingly.

"Water's boiling."

"Hmm?"

He points to the stove and she follows with her gaze. The noodles are foaming over the side.

"Shit!" She removes the lid and lifts the pot from the heat. The boys titter with laughter. "No one repeat that."

"Repeat what?" Jax asks, eyes gleaming.

"Nice try."

When the noodles are calm again, she checks the sauce, only to find it was turned to high instead of low. The bottom has burnt. She sighs and synchronously stirs both pots in rhythm with the second hand on the clock, counting down toward the moment when she can be off duty.

She lets the boys test the noodles. Den eats one and Jax practices making his stick to the wall. Satisfied, she turns off both burners with emphasis. The steam from the noodles stings her arms as she holds the lid to let them drain. She resists the urge to move and simply withstands the pain.

She plates three servings with noodles and sauce, careful to serve the boys the smooth unburnt portions. She scrapes the pot and plates her own with the crunchy red film, once a delicious homemade sauce. She sprinkles the tops with freshly shredded parmesan and adds a garnish of sliced olives and cherry tomato halves, just like Eric would have done. Although he'd never have served crunchy sauce. A hollow ache creeps into her chest. She sidesteps it and carries the plates to the table.

It becomes clear that, rather than algebra, Den has covered his paper with doodles of anthropomorphized vegetables and a knife—dressed as a magician—sawing them in half. She serves his plate along with raised eyebrows and a head tilt, the expert mom-look that says *really?* He shoves the page under his math book and tosses his gaze to the ceiling.

Jax smirks. "You want some butter with those rolls?"

Laura laughs and elbows Den in the arm. She high-fives Jax. The math-avoider just rolls his eyes even harder.

Laughter and (mostly) harmless insults ping pong between the boys as Laura settles into her own seat. She continues to laugh along with them, sips down two Advil with her wine, and breathes deeply. Jax grabs her phone and puts on their favorite Spotify play-list—lovingly titled *Dad Jams*—featuring Eric's favorite songs. REO Speedwagon streams in the background and the trio lift and tink their plates together as though in a toast before digging in.

Her sons' conversation muffles in her ears as she spools her noodles around her fork. She peeks at the clock on the wall, its hands gently reminding her only two more hours and she can disappear. After dinner.

They finish eating and Jax says, "Let's play a game?"

Den smirks and pulls out his doodle page. "No, thanks."

"You can pick."

"No."

"Come on, please?"

"No."

"Mom? Pleeeeease?"

"How about ice cream?" she says.

"Yes!" they say.

She clicks her tongue. "But, only if we play a game."

Den immediately rolls his eyes again but Jax laughs and cheers.

"Fine. Three scoops. Plus chocolate syrup and whip cream. And it has to be Uno or Phase 10. No Monopoly."

"Deal!" Jax says.

They all overload their bowls, Laura more for show than to actually eat, and play Phase 10. At some point it's clear that Den's actually enjoying himself. Laura smiles, thinking how much he looks like Eric.

They finish the game—Jax has put them to shame—and create an assembly line of wash-rinse-dry for the dishes. Eric's absolute favorite song—"Bohemian Rhapsody"—comes on. Jax croons into the wooden spoon. Laura laughs and swirls the suds around the dish before passing it to Den, who shakes his head with older brother superiority, refusing to sing along. He's able to ignore Jax's infectious tonal inflections but can't resist the rock-out part. Den head bangs in rhythm and air guitars a skillet. Laura is doubled over in laughter with suds up to her elbows.

When the song hits that slow final line, both boys are crooning in unison and pretending to play the final notes on their imaginary instruments. Their epic finale ends as they fall into a pile of laughter on the kitchen floor, tears streaming down their faces. Laura towels her arms dry and helps them to their feet, her sides hurting from laughter but her heart hurting from grief. Seeing the boys let loose together makes Eric come alive, and it's almost too much to bear.

She makes a silent plea a second before she looks at the clock. 8:30 at last.

"Okay, you two. I'll finish the dishes. You go do jammies and brush teeth. Then you can play video games for a bit before bed, if you promise to read for twenty minutes in the morning."

They shout a joyous, "Yes!" and run upstairs.

Once they are out of sight, she exhales and leans over the counter, hiding her face in her arms, a solitaire version of heads-up seven-up—the only one picked but still guaranteed to lose.

The music cuts out and silence dumps on her like cold water. She startles and checks her phone. *Are you still there? We don't want to play to an empty room?* The hollow ache returns along with fatigue. She closes the app and finishes the remaining few dishes in silence. Upstairs the boys are yelling and laughing. She wants to smile but her face is heavy, too heavy to do anything but exist.

She switches the laundry and carries folded piles to the boys' room. She puts them away like books with their spines out, Kondomari-style, and arranges them according to the colors of the rainbow: ROY to the north, BIV to the south, and G the equator.

She kisses the boys and tells them she is going to take a bath. "Light's out by 9:30."

"Yes, Mom," they say without looking up from the TV.

Once behind her bathroom door, she lets out a long, tired sigh of relief. She starts the bathwater in the garden-sized tub, adjusting the temperature until it's hot to the touch, and then drips lavender oil into the churning water. The steam carries the scent up to her and she inhales, the promise of her soothing escape only moments away.

She undresses, trying not to catch sight of her too-thin body and sagging mom boobs in the mirror. Her husband would have made her look, would have traced her skin and reminded her how beautiful she is. Instead, she stands naked on the bathroom rug, arms wrapped around herself, watching the water rise. On the wall above the tub hangs her husband's favorite painting, the one she was working on when they met. She faces away from it intentionally, but she knows it as intimately as she knows her own body. Every stroke.

A lone figure in a field beneath a cloudy sky. The being's body geometric and peculiar, built from fiery oranges and reds. The vibrant green of the field beneath its elliptic limbs. The blue sky above obstructed by patches of bulbous clouds. Surrounded by beauty but alone.

The water reaches its peak height and she shuts off the faucet. She plunges in her right foot, sucking air through her teeth at the scalding temperature, followed by her left. Hands grasping either side of the tub, she lowers herself slowly into the stinging heat. She's halfway in, the water line now at her belly button, when a knock rattles from the bathroom door. The suddenness of sound breaks her concentration and she slips, submerging the rest of her body instantly into the lavender lava she so delicately prepared. Water splashes up and over the sides of the tub onto the tile floor.

She shrieks and then silence falls on both sides of the door.

"Mom?" says a voice. It's Den.

"Yeah?" she answers. Her reply breathless, skin stinging.

"Can you come here?"

"What do you need, buddy?"

"I don't feel very good."

She closes her eyes, doing her best to breathe deeply and not cringe with annoyance. "Sorry, dude. It was probably the spaghetti. Just go lie down. I'll come check on you when I'm done."

No reply.

"Okay?"

"Okay."

She waits, listening, but no footsteps trod away from the door. "Honey, are you still there?"

"Yeah."

She frowns and waits a beat, but he says nothing. With a sigh, she pushes herself to her feet. The air chills her instantly, signaling goosebumps despite the steaming water cascading from her skin, and leaves her feeling exposed. She steps out—cautiously so as not to slip on the now-sopping floor—and throws down a towel, shifting it with her feet to soak up the puddles. She cinches her robe tightly around her and opens the door.

Den stands with slumped shoulders, not meeting her eye. He's already eclipsed her in height, so she dips her head and looks up at him. At first she thinks he looks guilty and her expression moves in for the mom-look again, but then she realizes. His squinted eyes. His tightened jaw and pinched lips. He's in pain.

"What's going on? Are you sick?" She feels his forehead and lifts his face so she can see in his eyes. They are red and teary. "Hey, what's the matter?"

He shrugs.

"Was my cooking really that bad?"

A grin twitches on his mouth and he nods.

She smiles. "You really don't feel good? Or is it something else?"

He nods again so she waits for him to share more.

"I miss Dad."

Her heart clenches in her chest. "Oh, sweetheart." She wraps her arms around him and he hides his face against her shoulder. "What brought this on? Did something happen?"

He shakes his head and buries it in her robe. A sob escapes and suddenly he's crying hard. She lifts her hands from his back in surprise and replaces them just as quickly.

"Okay. It's okay." She sways slowly, rubbing one hand over his hair and the other on his back, humming in rhythm. In her mind he is a tiny baby, only a week old, small enough to curl up between her collar bone and breast. She catches sight of their strange slow dance in the mirror and smiles. Not so little anymore.

His breathing slows and the shudders soften. A stray drip from the faucet falls into the bath with a plunk. He sniffs loudly and releases his grip, standing straight. His eyes are even redder now, but the spitting image of his father.

"Can we snuggle in your bed until I fall asleep, you know, like we used to?"

Laura glances at her filled-to-the-brim bathtub, ready and waiting, and then to the painting hanging above. Alone but surrounded by beauty.

She smiles softly, turns back to her son, and sweeps the too-long hair from his eyes. "Sure, sweetie. Hop in and I'll be there soon." She smiles wider as his lanky form climbs under the covers.

Alone behind the bathroom door once more, she steps to the tub. This time she reaches in with her hand, pulls the cord, and lets it drain.

. . . . . .

She doesn't exactly sleep well that night, with not one but two not-so-little-anymore sons snuggling against her in bed. She lies awake, staring at their lanky, awkward bodies snoozing beside her as she thinks of the last three years and all they've gone through. Then she imagines all the time stretching out in front of them left to be lived. Carefully, she tucks the unruly hair out of each of their faces and gives them each a kiss. Then she simply basks in rays of her beautiful children.

Her best, unfinished work.

WORLDVIEW

ELIXIR

Written by Julia Blair
Edited by Catherine Lunardon

"Give me your opinion, Fleur. I can't tell a Marseille red from trough water with this cold."

I was born with a rare talent, you see, one shared by my uncle Phillippe, the Master of Wine to the Lord of Brancion. A nose, he calls it, and indeed we share that same crooked feature, though I like to think my own nose is somewhat more petite than his bulbous snout. Growing up amid the vineyards of Bourgogne, my unusual palate was noticed at an early age when I could identify from which climate our table wine came, whether the year had been dry or wet, and even how long it had aged from harvest to table. Since coming to the chateau at twelve to help my aging uncle, I'd thanked our good Lord every Sunday and holy day for blessing me with such a gift. It kept me well away from household drudgery, at least until I married.

I took the cup from my uncle and silently appealed to Holy St. Morand, whose icon overlooked these cellars. In my hand I held a draw from this year's harvest, the first I'd attended from vine to keg. Within this cup I hoped to taste the essence of a fine Chardonnay.

These are the markers of a good wine: the scent of broom and white roses, of verbena and green forest fern at the height of summer. It should be full and balanced, with a finish of pine and fennel, and a buttery smoothness meant to be savored. Such qualities comprise a vintage worthy of the Brancion mark and I prayed to find them now.

I closed my eyes and sipped.

At once I shook my head and spat into the bucket near my uncle's feet. "Too tart. Too much depth to the acid. Not ready for the high table."

Uncle Phillippe sneezed, wiped his nose on his sleeve, and we moved along the row of casks. His voice was thick and phlegmy. "It will age well, I wager. Time will give it depth and character." His lantern cast a wavering light as we walked through the cool cellar. He rapped his knuckles, raising dust from another barrel. "Tell me what you think of this one, my dear."

I extracted a small amount of pale liquid into my cup and once again began the appraisement I'd learned by his side. I sank into my senses to discover this wine's character, its clarity against the light, and its bouquet in the bell of my cup. A sip to hold against the palate, a second one to wash past teeth and cheeks, each spat in turn, and a final breath through the nose and mouth to capture lingering afternotes.

Uncle watched me carefully and I nodded. "It's quite good. A full-fruited nose and a smooth mouth. This is the German white. Isn't it?"

"The last of it." He sneezed again and hawked into the slop bucket. I hid my grimace. Once more he rapped the keg and I could hear the hollow within. "The angels have taken more than their share. These staves aren't as sound as your Jean makes them.

Following him back the way we'd come, I wondered what other cask might serve the guests tonight when the '84 ran out. I felt certain it would. I'd seen the list for tonight's celebration. It seemed that every lord and lady in the entire valley was invited to the princess's sixteenth birthday. This time, it was whispered, the king had taken great care not to leave anyone out.

Uncle wheezed at the top of the cellar stairs and leaned against the wall.

"Let me help, Uncle," I told him. "I can ready the glassware for service. You should rest."

Mopping beads of sweat from his face, he smiled at me. "Perhaps I will, but I must tell LaFitte. He doesn't care for surprises at any time, much less a grand event like this."

I left him and made my way through the back halls, empty but for an old woman whose arms were filled with fine linen. I didn't know her, but she stopped me as I passed.

Her back was bent, and she had to look up to meet my eye. "I fear I'm lost, child. I've these fancies for her ladyship, and I don't know the way."

I knew the chateau well, having served here for years. "The ladies' solar is this way and up another stair, mistress."

She went on in a grumble. "I spent all night at my needle and the whole morning to walk up the hill. Why there is no weaver's hall like any other decent household, I don't understand."

I shrugged. I didn't know myself, but it had always been that way. "If you'd like, I can run them up for you."

"You've a kind heart, child." She nodded. "You'll get little reward for it now, but it may come to you in time. No, I must take these up myself. I've a message for her ladyship."

"God keep you then, Grandmother."

Her dry chuckle echoed as she made her way up the stone staircase.

The kitchen was a madhouse when I arrived. Footmen dashed between pantry and hall, laden with table linens. Steward LaFitte shouted at the head cook, who berated a red-faced boy for plucking a hen too near the cheeses. The boy slunk outside with his half-plucked bird. The spit-boy stuck out his tongue at the other, stopping only when confronted with Cook's threatening fist.

"Jean's looking for you," said my friend Jenny when she spied me. Her nimble fingers rolled and shaped pastry dough without a pause.

I paid her no mind. Jean would have to wait. I made a space for myself at the cistern trough to wash the cellar dust from my hands.

Having done with the cook, the steward's attention fixed upon me and I saw him scowl. What had vexed him, I wondered, the lack of a suitable wine or that I had offered to help my uncle this night? Perhaps both.

LaFitte was the bridge between those who sat at the high table and those whose livelihoods were given to serving them. We were no mean country fief. The Lord of Brancion owed allegiance to none and ranked as high as any king in France. There was an expectation of excellence and pride in the work of those who delivered it. My Uncle Phillipe produced some of the best wine in the region; I had learned much at his side. Yet though LaFitte allowed my presence, I had still to prove my worth in the household. If I pleased him, he might be my ally, but even a small error might set him against me.

"What do you suppose Jean wants?" Jenny teased. She would not let it go.

I dried my hands on my pinafore. "Whatever it is, he'll have to wait."

"Your cheeks are red as a rose!" Jenny laughed. "I'll be your maid of honor before St. Stephen's Day!"

Jean found me some time later in the butler's pantry. I'd taken the bossed tumblers from their velvet-lined chest and was now polishing the pale green glass to a diamond brilliance.

"Good news, my sweet flower," he hummed in my ear.

I ducked his bold attempt to kiss me and frowned in reprimand. "Unless you've come to help me, I doubt it." I flicked my polishing rag at the legions of fine beakers awaiting my attention, row upon row, like soldiers awaiting battle. Beyond them stood their generals, heavy silver pitchers into which Uncle would decant tonight's wine, at least while it lasted.

He looked around in doubt. "Come outside and sit with me a moment. I'm to return to the village and haven't much time."

"Nor I, Jean Marchión, if I'm to stay in my uncle's good graces."

Jean's sunburned face split into a wide grin. "That's the thing, Fleur! I'll be made a journeyman on Michaelmas!"

I had known Jean Marchión all my life, and once his apprenticeship was over, it was expected by both of our families that we would marry. Betrothed even before I'd begun to help my uncle, there was no doubt by any reasoning it was a good match. Jean was not handsome, but he was fair and kind. Nor was I a great beauty, with my oversized nose.

I should be happy at his news. It had been a long time coming. I smoothed my hands down the rumpled linen of my workday dress and looked up to see his face fall.

"We can be married now. I had hoped you would share my joy." His voice was quiet when he spoke, reminding me that his mild temper was a quality as precious in a husband as my nose was to a winemaker. He took my hand and pressed a folded paper into it. "Father Bernard has written out our bans. It only needs your mark."

"I did not expect this so soon," I said, tucking the packet into my pinafore. "Let us talk tomorrow." Blinking, I turned from him and returned to polishing the glassware. To my ears came first his gusting sigh and then his fading footsteps on the stone flags.

Ah, what had I done?

I had little time to dwell upon it. As soon as the glasses were whisked away to the footmen's station, LaFitte pressed me into service folding canapes in the kitchen. "You've done well enough. Now leave the wine to Phillippe," he muttered. "We are shorthanded here." Uncle was nowhere in sight and I fretted there would be nothing in store when the German white ran dry.

By the time I was released from duty, my fingers cramped and my back ached. I didn't know how Jenny could do this day after day, yet her eyes still sparkled and her smile was quick as I fled the kitchen for the terraced garden.

It was almost as hot outside as in, despite the late season. The kitchen garden swelled with its bounty. I stood at the balustrade looking down from the heights. On the slopes below, the vines had long surrendered their gold for the newest vintage of the Chateau's remarkable wine.

A lone rider trotted down the dusty service road to Brancion, lanky Jean on his mule, all elbows and knees. I could not see myself as the wife of any other, and our few kisses warmed me in a way I dared not confess to Father Bernard. Jean's work as a barrel maker would bring steady income to our family, but it kept him in the village, beside the river where his master's goods were easily sold and shipped. It meant the end of my time as my uncle's assistant, where I was a part of the winemaking from vine to table, from hill to the high hall. I loved it, and I knew I could not live in both worlds. It was foolish of me to think otherwise.

I made my way to a stone bench. It was warm through my skirts, and the afternoon sun filled the terrace with honeyed light that reminded me of the deep gold one sees in the very best chardonnays. Bees buzzed in late-blooming flowers. The rich scent of fallen leaves and fallow earth filled my nose. Soon enough, I'd be back at work, for Uncle was too sick to decant and chill the wine for service.

Tomorrow I would go to the village and speak with Jean. My stomach trembled thinking of my father's wrath at the loss of my dowry. I would be disowned, at best.

For now, I cast consequence to the wind and settled back against the warm stone wall. As I drowsed, I felt as though I floated in a cup of golden wine. Dappled sunshine painted the folds of my skirt. The very air seemed to sparkle with effervescence. My limbs felt heavy and loose, and my eyes began to droop. It seemed far too much effort to hold them open.

Just a small nap, I told myself. A few minutes more and then back to work. I closed my eyes and gave a sigh that lingered in my ears.

. . . . . .

I came awake with a start. The light was different now, clear and pale and casting shadows to the west. The air seemed cooler too, and everything was quiet. Had I slept through the night?

I leaped to my feet and was jerked back hard by my hair. Dry leaves rattled from my lap. My hand flew upward to find thorny brambles tangled in my plait. They pinched and pricked as I pulled at them. All about me stood a garden in neglect. Overgrown vines braided across paths, and mounds of brown leaves banked against the walls. Pumpkins and courgettes were withered husks still on the vine. Buzzing angrily, fat bumblebees crept from beneath dead leaves to launch themselves unsteadily into the cool morning air.

For it *was* morning. I could not deny the midmorning sun peeping over the high garden walls. *Had the seasons turned? How long had I slept?*

From the kitchens, I heard a sharp crack and a rising wail. Stumbling, I ran in that direction, cramped from sleeping upright against cold stone. The path was overgrown and long-neglected. I stubbed a toe against a gnarled root I knew had not been there when I came out. I grew more uneasy with every moment.

Outside the open door, the kitchen boy was slumped on his stool, slack-mouthed with sleep. Still clutched in his hands was a half-plucked hen. I saw the boy jerk awake, blinking comically. Our eyes met and I was sure his confusion mirrored my own.

I barged into the kitchen hall to see folk waking, some still frozen midway through tasks, others standing dazed. The spit-boy's ragged wails subsided and he cradled his cheek in hand. He looked up with wet eyes at Cook, who stared at her own raised fist as though she'd never seen it before. The hog had burned slightly on one side. I watched with a growing sense of unease as the glowing coals on the hearth beneath it burst into sudden flames. The spit-boy leaped back, frightened. Beside the ovens, Jenny's eyes flew open and she dropped the plate in her hand with a crash. Voices rose, cracked with disuse, and questions flew faster than the flies that began to buzz up from the windowsills.

Cook looked about and crossed herself. "What is going on here?" she demanded in a voice that cut through the rising murmur. "Get back to your work! All of you!"

Her command restored a sense of normalcy in the face of something inexplicable. Scullery maids commenced scrubbing pots, grumbling that the wash water had gone cold. Jenny crouched to clean up pottery shards and shattered tarts. With a rough shove from Cook, the spit-boy resumed turning the great carcass.

Into this odd scene of people awkwardly taking up forgotten chores, the steward burst into the kitchen.

"Listen to me!" he cried out. "I have orders from the king!"

Faces turned toward him.

"The princess is to be married! This is to be a wedding feast instead!"

All about were questions and cries of bewilderment, but LaFitte was quick to explain.

"We have been in an enchantment—yes, it's true—broken by a foreign prince, who now exchanges holy vows with the princess." LaFitte's face showed strain as the strange news tumbled from his lips. "We must outdo ourselves tonight. Spare no effort!"

As if to underscore his urgency, the chapel's great bell began to toll and the kitchen staff once again exploded into action. Better to think now of the labors at hand than to contemplate the nature of enchantment.

LaFitte pulled me aside. "Where is Phillippe? He's not given me his selection. Find him, girl. I've other things to see to."

I hadn't seen my uncle since awaking in the garden, and I began to wonder how long that stolen nap had been.

I flew down the twisting cellar stairs and flung open the heavy door. "Uncle!" I cried out. "Uncle Phillipe!"

In response came a stifled moan. I found my uncle collapsed beside a wooden bench. Crouching beside him, I turned his gray face to mine. His skin felt cool and clammy beneath my fingers. I helped him to sit up. "Rest, Uncle. I'll bring you some water."

"Fleur," he rasped, his fingers closing on my sleeve as though he pulled grapes from the vine. "Jean came to me this morning. You must follow your heart."

"Yes, Uncle," I said as tears stung my eyes.

His voice hitched and wheezed. "It is the only thing that matters."

He drew in a broken breath and let it go in a great exhalation. His eyes closed and his head was heavy in my hands.

"Uncle! Uncle! Please!" I cried.

I heard the clatter of feet on the cellar stairs

"Dear God! Phillippe!" LaFitte knelt beside me and pressed his hand to my uncle's slack cheek.

I was already weeping when the steward declared him gone. I crossed myself and prayed to Our Lord for his soul.

LaFitte laid a hand on my shoulder. "I will have him put in my room and the priest summoned."

I crumpled a corner of my apron and pressed it to my eyes.

LaFitte's grip tightened. "Fleur, can you—you must take over for him. Our service tonight must be above reproach. I fear for my place, for all of us, with a new lord in a world we no longer know."

I nodded my assent though I'd no idea what to do. "How long," I asked, "did we sleep?"

"A hundred years," he whispered. He closed his eyes, his face constricting. "God save us, it has been one hundred years."

For a moment the floor seemed to dip and sway beneath me. How could it be true? I looked at my uncle. His poor heart had given out. It was a wonder he'd woken at all. *A hundred years!* My thoughts wheeled like birds above a threshing field, but I pushed them away. Uncle must be tended to, and then there was the matter of wine.

With LaFitte gone to fetch the priest, I gently straightened the collar of my uncle's smock. In death, his face was no longer lined. With his eyes closed and his hands resting on his chest, he truly looked to be asleep. But asleep for an eternity this time.

The priest arrived, accompanied by two footmen. I followed as they laid my uncle's body on a pallet in LaFitte's small room. I stayed a moment longer to listen to the priest begin his prayers and then bid my uncle farewell.

The bustle in the kitchen had reached a fevered pitch. I was glad to return to the quiet of the cellar.

They had not yet taken up the keg of German white from earlier that day. I stopped myself. That day had passed a hundred years ago. At any rate, there was not enough of it to last an evening's revelry. No, the only thing we had in sufficient quantity was this summer's Chardonnay and it was much too young.

Or was it?

It was hard to know what had been affected by the enchanted sleep and what had not. The garden was overgrown, but the roast on the spit still dripped fat into the fire. Not a one of us had grown old, yet my poor uncle's heart could not bear the passage of so many years. A layer of dust flurried beneath my feet as I walked down the aisle I had swept only this morning.

I reached the kegs of the chateau's youngest vintage and took a cup from the shelf. The bung was stiff but I persisted until it loosened and then piped a sample into my cup.

Although late afternoon when I'd fallen asleep, it was a spring morning now and the cellar was flooded with soft light from the high windows. I held the glass up to the sunlight and swirled it slowly. No sediment marred the pour, and the wine itself was the same heartbreaking gold of that autumn afternoon a century past.

I brought the glass to my face, closed my eyes and inhaled. My nose burst with the aroma of citrus and autumn fruit. I could not help but smile.

And then I sipped and was rewarded by a mouth so fine my tears sprang again. I could taste the sun on the fields and the flinty minerals of the soil. I could taste the passage of years. The full lives and mourned deaths of those with whom I'd toiled in the vineyards, of everyone I'd known who had worked and loved, grown old and died. It was not just wine. It was the sum of all that I held most dearly to my heart, my family, my friends, and the land itself.

It was my life.

. . . . . .

The wedding feast unfurled without flaw, at least as far as those nobles in attendance knew. For us in the back halls and kitchens of the chateau, broken glasses were swept up and burned bits were trimmed from roasts. My wine selection was well-received, and not even the champagne could hold a candle to the "young" chardonnay.

I saw the princess too, but only from a distance. With her was the prince who had come upon us while we slept. They seemed untouched by the world around them, like creatures from a fairy tale, the kind my dear mamán told me when I was a child. I watched from the shadows of the hallway entrance until the candles sparkled in the chandeliers, the minstrels tuned their lutes and flutes, and the pavane began.

The sky, when I slipped outside to the terraced garden, was a breathtaking blue, pale near the horizon and darkening overhead like a pool of still water. On the distant highway folk were still coming and going, latecomers to the celebration as well as those who wanted to see for themselves this enchanted chateau upon whose slopes now lay a tangle of rose briar and thorn.

While the light remained, I looked beyond them to Brancion, the village where I had been born. It was as if I looked upon a childhood playmate now grown—an old friend dressed in unfamiliar clothes. A tall church tower that had not been there this morning a hundred years ago now rose from the plaza. A perplexing web of paths and lanes extended beyond familiar bounds, and new cottages and shops clustered where once had been a water meadow. I traced the river but could not find Jean's barrel shed.

Follow your heart, my uncle had said. Even before I had fallen asleep, I had resolved to do that very thing, that on the morrow I would disappoint my family and break the heart of a man who deserved much better. But now, I thought, there would be no family for me. With my uncle gone, my family name would have passed with my father, for I had only sisters. Either way, Jean would not have waited for me, and even if he did, I would never have come in his lifetime.

One hundred years had passed while I slept, and the guilt that had niggled me when I began this day had been swept away, as inconsequential as dust on flagstones.

I pulled Jean's letter from my pinafore, now brittle and crumbling in my fingers. The evening breeze rose as the sun sank behind the hills. I listened to it whisper and let it pull the bits of paper from my fingers to fall like withered petals on the briars below.

These are markers of this day—the things I will remember.

A true heart too easily broken. The seductive warmth of an autumn afternoon. The acrid scent of cellar dust and my uncle's sad eyes upon me. And the golden notes of a wine as pure as a sacrament.

TAKE THE NEXT STEP

Now that you've read examples of core events for each of the twelve content genres, it's time to go deeper and discover how they work at the beat level. The companion *Contender Guide* does just that.

It analyzes the stories you've just read from a Story Grid Editor's perspective, following Shawn's example from the GYC course materials. Each story is broken down into a spreadsheet with the progression of beats and how each affects the overall story. For even more examples, check out the GYC course.

The Story Grid Universe, like the literal universe, is constantly expanding. As Shawn continues to chart new territory on his exploration of stories, so, too, does the community grow and create together using these new tools. In this forward movement, we believe in *proving the value of using these tools* (which is why this Anthology exists) and *welcoming others to join us on the journey.* That means you, doing the work with us.

As this Universe grows, there will be more opportunities to level up and showcase powerful stories that work. Visit storygrid. com/publishing/ to find out more about how you can help us elevate the stories we tell and share your work with us.

Everything in the Story Grid Universe is designed to help make you a better writer. Taking up the challenge is up to you.

We hope you do.

KIMBERLY KESSLER is a Story Grid Certified Editor, TEDx speaker, and one-fourth of the Story Grid Editor Roundtable Podcast. As an editor, she specializes in crafting authentic character arcs and internally driven stories. As a novelist and filmmaker, she uses humor as a means to cope with and explore trauma—ultimately, so we can find a redemptive perspective on pain. She lives in Washington state with her stand-up comedian husband and three "think they're a comedian" kids. You can connect with her directly at www.kimberkessler.com.

REBECCA MONTERUSSO is a writer and certified Story Grid editor who's attended two McKee seminars, hosted workshops at Barnes and Noble, and self-published a nonfiction book on writing. She produces a podcast called A Story That Works and currently creates content for ROI Online. Her writing has been featured on Havok, Jane Friedman, The Creative Penn, and DIY MFA. She's a pretty good crocheter, avid reader, amateur graphic designer, and loves traveling the world. Short story is currently her favorite medium for writing fiction. You can find out more at www.creativitythroughconstraints.com.